The triggers of psychosis pulled.

I0553391

A novel

By Jesse Morris

Copyright TXu 1-938-542

August 18, 2014 Jesse Morris

Robert Tuttle Morris, world renowned surgeon, as early as 1877 said that all truly great writers wrote how they did, due to the influence of bacterial toxins present in their brain. I have been reading books my entire life. That is a shared psychotic disorder. I spent 7 years in complete isolation reading for 16 to 20 hours a day and had no other contact with this world. I could describe to you in detail the behavioral patterns of every major writer who has lived for the last 3000 years. I could tell you what they ate, what they drank, what they looked like, what they wrote, and what they said, if they said anything.

I have been in an institution for 10 years. I shot someone accidentally. Recently, about 3 months ago, I tried to kill myself. I was told by one of the nurses that I stabbed myself 12 times in the neck, and that, both doctors agreed, I had seriously attempted to end my life and didn't just want attention. The place that I am at now, is a close management mental- health facility. One of my new psychiatrists, a young woman, has urged me to begin writing in this journal. She explained to me in depth the therapeutic benefits of releasing negative thoughts and feelings by writing about them. Which, I am now typing almost a year later in a different institution.

There is an inmate in this unit who I have been watching very closely for some time. He has agreed to tell me his life story and that is going to be the subject matter of this story, as it is a biographically historical matter. Initially, he told me that his name was Heath Letcher. Thee, Heath Letcher. The one and only. But only several seconds passed by, after he told me his name, before he grinned, and then began laughing. After which, he stood up very seriously, and looked around the unit as if he were, angry, then suddenly he struck his right arm up into the air, into a Nazi salute, with his index finger pointed straight up, and then, he swung it around and poked himself directly in his rectum and then began laughing again, almost hysterically, and at that point he continued to yell out that he was Heath Letcher, and that he was ahead of the curve, much further ahead than others could in fact, speculate about. He was then subdued. I have received injections myself and have been told that thorozine is used. I have asked several of the nurses in here about the effects of thorozine and the dosage that they are using and have been told that everything is, alright, and that I didn't need to worry.

Heath, as he insists to be called, used the word psychopathology when we were talking, just the other day; in reference to myself, in one of our conversations, about something I had brought up that was on the world news. I had never given much thought to that word, or to its meaning. Yet, Mr. Letcher told me, that to understand him, and or, psychopathology, I would have to go through a psychopathological phase, in which certain neurological triggers would be pulled. That I would have to change, once again, irrevocably, and that my telomeres would be shortened, irreversibly. A change in which, as often occurs in natural enviornments, an organism could no longer return to what it was previously.

ALL OF THIS BEGAN JUST A FEW WEEKS AGO. Before a certain event happened. Previously, Mr. Letcher was known only as; that little queer, as one old man described him to me. Out of 67 inmates in this unit no one else had a comment about him. You don't get a lot out of people in this place, but if you are reading this you can see the environmental effects of this habitat in their movements, and in their behavioral patterns. We are only allowed to watch the public broadcasting channel. ALL OF THIS BEGAN WHILE THE WORLD NEWS WAS ON.

A young man, out of the blue Mr. Letcher said, as the television program would like you and I to believe, a young man, who appeared to be gifted, and promising, murdered 12 people and injured a hundred more during the premiere night of a film. That is what your story is about, Mr. Letcher said. Precisely because the government won't give in to their own inclinations, because no one will be honest, he insisted, about the connections that should have been discussed, in depth, immediately after the shooting, and the fingers that should have been pointed, between the young man and the subject matter of the film he desecrated. Or the young man, perhaps having been completely inspired by the film director's previous film, or the film directors psychiatric state himself, well, he said, and then I witnessed him run directly up to an overweight Hispanic inmate and he bit down directly into the top of his head. I believe that he bit into the fellow's scalp as hard as he could and blood immediately began streaming down both sides of its head and it could be heard screaming up to 400 yards away. Shortly thereafter Mr. Letcher was subdued. The last thing I heard him say that evening, was that, he wouldn't stop until the director, and the other English fellow as well, WERE HELD ACCOUNTABLE. He yelled out that he didn't care about the metal table and the motor cycle helmet, or the strait jacket, or the chair, and that he would kill someone before it was over with and then he was injected.

When he came back. . . . . for an entire day he was quiet, and I am sorry for it.

His eyes were a bit, puffy, like the way I write. Occasionally he would make a sound similar to that of an owl; whooing. A sort of whoo, whoo. He would look around, slowly, suddenly, then appear absent once again. It was at that time that I began to take an interest in this person. Heath, Letcher. I began to feel differently about a lot of things. To type any of this, at this present moment, also, makes me feel very anxious, and uncomfortable. The medication I take every evening, I am sure, is part of the reason why I have not been feeling like myself. There are people in here with physical disfigurements, crooked and rotting teeth, baldness, obesity, green skin, an all- around harrowing stench. Yet, I do not have any of these problems.

Mr. Letcher was cheerful again two days later. All day, inconspicuously, I witnessed him tormenting several of the inmates in this unit. By passing gas while standing right beside someone. Or, when absolutely no one else was looking, licking someone's ear. I saw him kiss one person on the forehead, the same one in fact, who had said that he was a little queer. On and on. Pleas for justice. Fairness. He could go on for years he told me, years, and never say a word to anyone. Never even look another person in the eye. But if he had done it, he wouldn't remember it. He wouldn't want to. If he had a choice, he said, he wouldn't want to remember anything, and he wouldn't talk to any-one. **But to write it down is different. Because out of the two ways of you seeing me do what is to follow, it is better for you not to see me, he said.**

Recently, I had been feeling depressed. **Very depressed.**
But, this morning I drank a large cup of coffee while I was talking
to one of my psychiatrists, and I suddenly feel better. Most of our
discussion was about Mr. Letcher, who, the psychiatrist
informed me was also one of her patients. The psychiatrist, a
Mrs. Kim, Jisoo Kim, a young south Korean woman, also claimed
that she had read my book. She stated that she writes frequently
herself and that she can help me to become a better writer, and a
better person. We discussed the recent shooting. In depth.
Aesthically. She was, as, interested in it as I was. I explained to
her that never in my life had I felt so uneasy about an incident
and that I felt that; the world was becoming highly
unpredictable, which previously I didn't believe due to the
geometrical similarities in all biological objects. She told me that
the world had always been unpredictable even if it was built, but
that I was just now realizing it because like me, the creator, and,
or, government, was in a state of infancy as well. Nothing
surprised her anymore in fact. She knew all about Mr. Nolman
and his films. A prestigious individual, she said. When I said his
name a scene of an emotionally distraught woman pushed over
the edge to hang herself because of the duality of her husband's
character immediately came to her mind. It was all very
intriguing she said, but sad. Mr. Nolman, she said, unfortunately
does not understand how many neurologically impaired

individuals are being influenced by his films. As a result of one person, actually, physically, being two. But no one else knowing it.

What do you think about sacrifice she asked me?

HAVE YOU HAD A CHOICE IN WHICH PARTS OF YOUR LIFE WERE SACRIFICED?

I felt then that she was alluding to my own suicide attempt. I told her that I would do it again if she thought it was funny. I then asked her if I could have another cup of coffee and she got up and returned moments later with a cup. Was I homosexual, she asked me? Had I ever shot anyone? Had I looked into the mirror lately? These were the only 3 questions she asked me during our first session. What was I thinking about she wanted to know? I asked her if she was married and she said that she wasn't. I asked her what she liked to do when she wasn't at work and she said sleep. I asked her what she thought about my book and she said that it was so disfiguring to the reader that 99 percent of the population would never understand it and the other 1 percent would find it boring. You are worse than Lautreamont she said. There are some people in this world who don't hate or fear anything. They have reached that, she told me. Is that how you are I asked her? She only shifted her hair in response. Never in my life have I met a person who was so unaware of their own self-image. Mr. Letcher told me that she allowed him to masturbate in front of her during their sessions. Which, would mean nothing, except for the fact that she would urge him on, and would even insult him for not going fast enough, and would accuse him of not taking her seriously also. And that last part bothered me. I even asked Mr. Letcher to clarify in what context she said it, and he told me that while she was running her fingers through her hair and was looking up at the ceiling, she would say very softly, you're not taking me seriously. Not yet.

Mr. Letcher despises psychologists and especially anyone who mentions Freud he emphasized, as Freud is out of date, but, said that she had Freudian type complexes. Which, probably originated in the last few years and not during her childhood and he agreed with me that she was highly unaware of her own behavior as most people are. Mr. Letcher then kissed me on the top of my head and told me that I was his brother. He insisted that we weren't in an institution but that we were on a penal colony off of the coast of French Guiana, and that he would pay for my escape. That we could very well never leave the room that we were in. Or Sarte's play either. If that wasn't the case, I was old man Karamazov and he was Dostoevsky. We were brothers, but we had to act like the same person, in order to make a living, no matter the consequences. Then he told me that he was in the institution for 12 counts of murder, and over 100 counts of attempted murder. He said that he had been severely abused as a child and that his acts of violence had been a product of the bidirectional influences of his childhood environment, and nothing more.

Ms. Kim, when confronted about her apparent lack of self-awareness in social settings, explained to me that such an idea was a waste of her time. That, there was no credible research indicating that there are benefits from prolonged self-analysis, and she also added, you never go looking for a monster anyway. She cited my own book and references I had made comparing all of the world's inhabitants to being parcels of one large biological organism and then told me how irrational I was but that I could be fixed. I lunged out at her at that point, I was sick of her already, and bit her. I was on top of her and was tearing her clothes off, it all happened so quickly and then, several guards rushed in and I was subdued. I remember how I felt after that injection, out of the hundreds, that I had deserved it.

For 36 hours they had me in the chair. I was sitting in front of the television and they walked up and grabbed me and then took me into the room with the chair and strapped me into it motionless. I sat there for 2 days and couldn't move. Not even my head. Then for three days I was in a strait jacket inside of a padded room after they had me in the god helmet. Mr. Letcher always gets strapped down on to a metal table that they have. He laughs the entire time. He says that it is kind and considerate of them to use the leather straps, and not metal straps with spikes. Some of the inmates in here either cannot talk or simply refuse to and so I have no choice but to talk to Mr. Letcher. Some of the inmates, if they don't come out of their rooms, Mr. Letcher spends lots of time with them. When he comes out of a room, if he spots me, he'll wink. Then begin laughing. It is a natural human restriction to accept the conditions of any environment Mr. Letcher explained to me, so why be so serious. You already know what catch 22 says, he said. About the rights of others. Every time they show the fellow from Colorado on TV in court Mr. Letcher has to be subdued by at least 9 Guards. Brilliance he will scream! Absolutely Brilliant!!!! He will scream so loud that most of the people in here will cover their ears and will cry out that they can't stand it. I'll get under a table, and crouch down like a rabbit, but I'll watch and listen, and I'll enjoy it, and giggle. The way that the fellow on t v nods, and dozes, and appears to not be to, here, nor there, that is exactly how I feel. A tragedy is happening, while it is being viewed and also happening at the same time. Only a neuroscientist could perceive the implications Mr. Letcher told me. A person living in a passive and highly submissive culture goes willingly to see a film in which the contents of their world will be challenged. Then, while the structure of their society collapses, and as a disfigured and subhuman villain takes over a large metropolitan city, as all of that is happening, suddenly there are gunshots and explosions, not only from the digital surround sound speakers but now also very close by. Then these people are actually massacred. They are watching human beings being shot on the screen in front of them, and then also around them in their immediate vicinity and some of them are actually shot themselves and never in the history of this world has such an event occurred. Except for the assassination of Lincoln, who was shot while watching a play, but it was a comedy, and he died while everyone was laughing. Mr. Letcher told me that he finds this all very disheartening, and humiliating, only because he believes that government intervention and restrictions on such films, and books, is eminent. Personally, I have been saddened, permanently, by the lives that were taken and felt that I had to do something about it, and do it quickly. It has tormented me and still does. Other shootings haven't affected me as this one has. For the most part, because I have never cried during a film except for one. I admire

Mr. Nolman. I really do. Still, like most people, he does not understand his own behavior, Mr. Letcher said.

Mr. Letcher told me that one of the inmates died in here this morning. He said that the inmate suffocated himself with a small amount of toilet paper. Mr. Letcher told me that he urged the inmate to do it. He told me to in fact write that down. That he had verbally persuaded another person to suffocate themselves. He had studied hypnosis in India. You can disassociate another person just by the act of writing alone, he told me. Reappearing, only in text can someone truly reappear, then, 3 guards approached us and subsequently told me that I was being released.

THE TRIGGERS OF PSYCHOSIS PULLED

What do you think Mr. Zuckenberg thinks about Jesse Eisenbert, Mr. Letcher asked me? That is a question. Do you think they've met? Surely, I told him. Surely they have met. That question plagues me, Mr. Letcher insisted. He told me to write down that whether they had or hadn't met plagued him, and what might have possibly been discussed, and how much of a put on it might have been, and if it was true that he had said it was raining outside or if that was just added into the script. Further, the question as to which of the two of them was more intelligent, made him dig at himself. Literally, with his nails. Who exactly was Jesse Eisenbert? Mr. Letcher wanted to know. He could have goggled him but refused to do so. The audacity. The despicable audacity to put on such a display of intelligence and contempt. It is to be scoffed at, but admitted Mr. Letcher explained. Mr. Letcher and I absolutely barked at each other, like dogs, for upwards of 30 minutes about mark zuckenbert and jesse eisenbert. Arguing the ins and outs of which of them was in fact the better man in this world. We were the final judges on the subject, no one else was worthy of it. In the end, I was all for mark. Mr. Letcher, favored jesse eisenbert, he said that jesse was headed down his path if he wasn't careful.

My new psychiatrist is another woman named Jisoo Kim. I haven't provoked anyone yet but would I told her. I have worms, and I hide under the table. That is all I would come clean about. I asked her about her shoes. They seemed cheap and out of place on an upscale psychiatrist, I can't remember if she said they were toms or tomtoms. She said she would find something better to wear if I didn't like them. They bothered me I told her, and I didn't want to see them again. She said that the medicine was helping me. She said that it would fix us and she didn't need a whistle either. Mr. Letcher insists that I redeem myself by writing about his life. He battled schizophrenia and was cured. He claims that he has out read me. But then, he stated, I was his pet and that he would fill me in on my literary shortcomings, and then he laughed for a moment and then, he licked around the inside of his lips like he did in the film, then just stared at me, inquiringly, then he laid down on my mattress and went to sleep. But stared directly at the wall for a few minutes before he did so.

For days on end, Mr. Letcher was quiet. He was changing, like you are, he said. He stared, but didn't blink as much as a normal person would. He sat in the same position for hours, and wouldn't flinch a muscle.

He wouldn't respond to my questions. He wouldn't eat. He wouldn't take his medicine, and was subdued. Was released. Found a chair again, sat, wouldn't do anything. Was subdued. Wasn't seen for a week, a year. Then, reappeared, right where he left off. Cheerful. Charming. Telling everyone how much he had missed them. Had been gone to India but was back. Wouldn't leave again. Although to me it had seemed like he had been gone for a very long time, I was also gone for a long period of time and can tell you that it goes by in a flash. What was happening in Colorado he wanted to know? At which point, upon being told, a certain story about, which, I fabricated, well, he barked, he howled, he ran around the unit in circles screaming and hollering and whacking people in the head as hard as he could and screaming; ILL DO IT YET! IF THEY DON'T LET HIM GO ILL DO IT YET, ILL KILL EVERYONE IN HERE! Then he was tackled and subdued.

While he was away I daydreamed constantly. I invented a person to talk to. A sort of goblin if you will. An old deformity. A person 3 feet in height, slightly fat, bald, and with a protruding forehead.

With a high pitched voice and unpleased with everything. An opionated grunt, who could be slapped or pinched and who would foam at the mouth at such treatment. Would cuss god, the government, and everything in between and would lash out and bite at the air and beat his chest and cry and would say he despised ever being born. This fellow and I did everything together. Anything loose, unattached, and able to fit into his mouth he would swallow. Nor could he pass by anything, anything at all, without touching it. He was constantly on the prowl, and for it, I treated him harshly. He was an irreproachable dog. He could be held and beat and he would squirm, and knaw, and squeal like a pig and I would laugh until I fell on the floor or was tackled by the guards and subdued. And in the event that I was tackled, by the guards, and injected, he would attack them and be subdued as well. We were strapped down on to two opposite metal tables facing each other and I cussed and threatened him for 48 hours straight and he cussed and threatened me back and he spat, grinded his teeth, and cussed me as if I were his dog, and in the event that I laughed, while he was cussing me, he would shake the table he was strapped to with all his might and would bang the motorcycle helmet and would scream and plead and beg for someone to come and cut my throat, or scream for someone to make that batch stop laughing. I had no name or title to him, I was a batch. Or I was, you mash, and said very sparingly and with contempt. He followed me around like a puppy and I took care of him. Sometimes, he had a habit of crawling around on his hands and knees like a child and when he did I would kick him for everything he was worth and he would scream and cry and cuss everything as I had never heard things spoken against in my life. Ms. Jisoo Kim said that this person was an unconscious projection of my past experiences and a positive sign of my recovery.

4 years ago I spent two years in complete isolation. With no sunlight. I was being housed under no human contact status. I was starved periodically and was given only given tea and bread that had been drugged. I lost my mind thousands of times. I pulled several of my own teeth out. When I was hungry I ate feces or roaches that I could catch. I chewed the ends of my fingers and legs. I pulled the hair out of my head and swallowed it whole. I bit my tongue repeatedly, in an attempt to remove it.

Mr. Letcher told me that I have holes in the back of my head with wires coming out of them and connecting into my lower back. He has a series of numbers on the bottom of his feet. He has been consistently telling me to; make sure you write that down. As have, the doctors, and the nurses as well. As I am a doctor. I have since been put on a new medication. My book, my last book, they say, has finally become a success. They showed me proof. It has sold over a million copies and I have ruined my life in the process. This was even before I began cutting myself out of all the pictures I had. Before I began rocking back and forth slowly. It is an effect of the medicine I have been told. It is dangerous to write this way if one is not, in fact, already mentally ill Mr. Letcher told me. Doctor or no doctor. He said that I didn't know what I was getting myself into, nor the reader. Although I had hanged myself, I wasn't mentally ill, but would become so. You're not even a decent writer after all, he told me, he was sure of it. He has read the first 15 pages of this journal and is sure. I clawed at his face, I tried to kill him in one stroke. I tore streaks of skin off of his face, and was beaten by the guards. His skin was still underneath my fingernails when they put me back in the isolation cell. The entire room is made out of green foam that you can only see until they close the door, so that you know in the future. There is no light at all or sound, yet, you see things and hear things as if they were happening right in front of you and you have no control over any of it. I knew, personally is the only word I can think of, that none of it was real and yet it continued. The midget paced the cell and lashed out occasionally as if he were infected with rabies, and scratched at himself. He would beat the padding and would plead hysterically for help. He kept a journal. One night as I was reading it I laughed at something he wrote and he attacked me and bit down hard on the end of my foot. I invented guards to subdue him so that I could have some peace. I reinvented the actor Heath Letcher, and jisoo kim also, to have people to talk to, and to torment. I replicated myself. A mirror image and I named this person the further. For instance; the further away from. The further interacted with these people and I watched. He was a sexual deviant and enjoyed torturing people. Occasionally, he would also lash out at me and I would have him subdued. One day, the further pulled one of my eyes out during a scuffle. An apparition in a suit urged him to do it, he said that I would see better in the dark with only one eye. I would be somewhere else, engaged in many activities, and then I would realize I was still in the isolation cell.

For months I cried several times a day, and thought about nothing other than how I could kill myself. I tried choking myself, starving myself, jumping up into the air and landing on my head, and many other schemes. The bean flap opened less frequently and I believe that I was only being fed two or three times a week. I was told to be quiet and not make a sound. Anytime the bean flap opened I cried out desperately to be killed, and was either hit or slapped on the mouth for saying so. I was told that I was being cured.

Teams of doctors evaluated my progress. I was put inside of a clear tank that hung from the ceiling of a massive laboratory. I was asked questions regarding my thoughts. I was monitored closely, and was woken up if I fell asleep. My blood was taken every day. My medications were rotated. I was transferred to an asylum. I was told that my mind would alter itself if I wore the helmet with all the wires coming out of it. I would die there if I didn't I was assured. Underweight. Overmedicated. Unknown. A shadow of who I was. I crept about. I was crippled. I degenerated. Some of my patients I kept in this state for years. After I wore the helmet I was released and put into a drug treatment program. I went back to college. I became a psychiatrist. I gained notoriety for the books I published on developmental and criminal psychology. And also; on the psychobiological processes occurring during acts of murder, suicide, and torture. I won the Nobel prize for literature. I was then asked to evaluate a neuroscientist who had no history of mental illness, no criminal record, and yet, who was claimed to have murdered a dozen innocent people out of the blue. I studied this case for months. I poured over it. The details of it consumed my waking life. I dreamed about it. I cried over it. I couldn't find anything. Absolutely not a thing helped me to understand why the young man committed the murders. I took him on and off a dozen different medications. I begged him and bribed him to no end. Nothing worked. He wouldn't speak. He wouldn't move. He stared. He dozed off. I concluded that he was a superhuman. I believed that he was missing part of his brain stem. Cat scans revealed that he had an enlarged prefrontal cortex. He was also a hermaphrodite, which was not revealed to the public, and my deepest inclination, my suspicion, was that he was a government test subject who had escaped from a facility in southeast Georgia. But that, he wouldn't spill the beans. Altogether I had no idea of what I was dealing with.

One day, after I had spent several hours crying at his feet for answers, he mumbled out, why so serious? At that moment I understood everything. I had suspected it, but didn't want to believe it, for Mr. Nolmans' sakes. Immediately I began to beat this person. I beat him to no end I assure you. I punched him, slapped him, kicked him, threw him into the wall, even sodomized him, slammed his head into the floor, tell me I told him, which one in fact made you do it. The second one, specifically, he stated. He was only waiting for the third film to be released. I continued beating him, I was on the urge of ripping the skin off of his face. Then, I wanted to know, had he seen the third film before its premiere night? He had. An internet bootleg site. I killed him. I beat his skull into the floor for several minutes until there were pieces of it. I was arrested and charged for his murder. My lawyers claimed that I was temporarily insane and I was found not guilty in trial but was taken into state custody, and to a mental health facility. Where I sit.

HOW ONE MEMORY REOCCURED SO PREDOMINATELY.

The length of memory.

Jisoo Kim continued to ask me if I had looked into the mirror lately.

I was still in the isolation cell.

Months had passed by, years perhaps, maybe close to a decade. I guessed, and yet I remembered nothing. My runt, who I had created, died and was lying in the corner of the room. I no longer ate anything. I drank water out of the toilet and nothing more. All at once, suddenly, I realized I was in a strait jacket. My ears began ringing. I had grown a very long beard, and I could feel mats of hair against my neck. Finally, I began to notice my own stench.

Heath Letcher said that I was dying but wouldn't die completely but wouldn't heal either. I couldn't even feel my eyes moving.

During my acceptance speech for the Nobel prize I explained that my book was in fact unnatural, in the purest form, and yet I had indulged in live human experiments for 8 years researching this new psychosis and found no evidence of neurotransmitter imbalances in my patients. No difference in f.m.r.i.s or petscans between healthy test subjects and my patients. Psychosis is innate and prearranged. It can be triggered. Given a set of very specific childhood circumstances of which I had coded. This new form of psychosis, the present form, the form I have, could go undetected for such a long period of time, because it was evolving. Then, as the older inmates began dying in our unit, the newer inmates, I realized, were increasingly becoming more aware of their symptoms. This led to new symptoms. I begged for more grants. I pleaded. I would need hundreds of thousands of dollars to research these new problems I was having. I wanted to inject my patients brain stems with embryonic stem cells. I also wanted the microbes that James Camhorn brought back from 7 miles below the ocean surface to inject into my own brain stem. One morning I received paperwork stating that in an unnamed government research facility a biological virus that had been formulated by the military was coded in 1999. This code would induce a permanent form of intense trepidation in which the test subject would reach a level of paranoia unprecedented and which would lead the individual to extremely organized acts of terror. This code, for experimentation purposes, has been transmitted into 4 films, of which 38 percent of the population of the United States has viewed. It effected roughly .08 percent of that subgroup. I had been in my apartment on a Sunday afternoon reading a new book on theoretical physics and model dependent realism when I was surrounded and subsequently kidnapped by 9 masked men.

I woke up in a padded room. I was told that I was to write a book on the behavior of psychiatrists and neurologists and the reasons for social catastrophes. I would be paid millions of dollars. I would be given my own compound and 4000 test subjects and would be left alone. I didn't trust them and so I agreed and as soon as I was let loose I fled. Moved to Russia. I bought a house outside of St. Petersburg and studied Russian literature for years before I shot myself in the head and lived. I lost my mind 8 thousand times in St. Petersburg. I became addicted to methamphetamine and didn't sleep for 40 days straight at least 23 times. I won 433 million dollars at the roulette table in Monaco. I bought planes, islands, compounds and a small paramilitary force. I had myself cloned. I drank coffee as one might consume a staple crop, snorted oxycodone 60s, ate absolutely nothing, fornicated like a Kentucky derby thoughourg bred and was finally hit with the baker act off of the coast of Naples while I was asleep on my yacht.

I was strapped motionless to a chair and had a feeding tube put down my throat and was left like that for 3 weeks. Heath Letcher asked me if I was responsible for the outcome of my adolescent personality? And my subsequent mental disorder? I was crushed with that question and at that point ceased to comprehend model dependent realism. What is there to understand about a system where one is merely an environmental output and has no say over their own development? Mr. Letcher wanted to know why his neural patterns revolved around the news media situation of the shooting and his medication and why he was in an institution and coming to a dead end stabbed himself 12 times in the neck, even though the report said that he overdosed on his medication.

The next day, the day after they let me out of the chair, Jisoo Kim wanted to know if I still heard voices inside my head? And how loud were they?

Somehow, at some point, I managed to jam the button in completely and from then on the water in my sink ran continuously. In a stream. My cortisol, serotonin, and adrenaline all fluxed in waves, I am sure, and I rolled around the padding in my room as a child might roll around in the grass in his backyard. I bit myself, repeatedly. I chewed on my arms, legs, hands and feet and howled, I am sure, like an injured wolf at the moon.

A year later I was put back into the unit with Heath Letcher. He introduced me to a new inmate named Christian Paleman. When I met him, Mr. Paleman weighed about 120 pounds, had sunken cheeks, and the majority of his bones could be seen, and not heard. He had once been a professional boxer, and had been a pillar of society, but had developed an extreme cocaine addiction out of sheer vanity and won an award for it. He was a rambunctious fellow, given to outbursts and sentiments that neither Mr. Letcher or myself combined were humanely capable of. I was afraid of this fellow immediately. The first time he was subdued it took a total of 12 guards to contain him and I slipped into a coma just at the sight of the incident. Mr. Letcher asked this fellow for his advice on how to write a book. At which point, he slammed his fist down on to the table. It must jump from subject to subject rapidly Mr. Paleman informed us in an authoritative tone. The modern populace is rash, unassuming, and irrational to the point of an elusive strain of insanity. The only way to get their attention, and hold it, is to present them with a higher degree of absurdity than their own and then to bombard them with loud noises, bright lights, and chaos in general on top of that. The more absurd the chaos, the more extremely unreasonable it is, the better. That is how Mr. Nolman and I have made our billions he informed us and then he slammed his fist down again. I am the product of the greatest 20th century circus act and I am now at the height of my powers. Then, immediately after he said that, he got up and walked into a nearby cell. Then, only seconds later, he reappeared upstairs on the second floor, by stepping out of another cell. This small miracle shocked Mr. Letcher to his core. There are two of them, Mr. Letcher told me, surely, he has a double. Nonsense, I said immediately, absolute nonsense. There is some other way he did it and I'm going to figure it out. No he has a double, or a twin, and that's all there is to it Mr. Letcher pleaded with me. That's entirely too simple I told him and I grabbed Mr. Letcher by his jumpsuit and I shook him as wildly as I could. He is not using a double and I am sure of it! Now you go and find out how he did it or I'll cut both sides of your mouth open.

On the psychology of Murder. That was the title of the book I had when I was in the isolation cell, even though there was no light for me to read it. I was told that I was in possession of it.

After a year without any caffeine Ms. Jisoo Kim gave me a large cup of coffee and this is the result. She explained to me that I was only imagining all of this, or of what happened, in my head and immediately I became more anxious at the possibility. I told her that I was still imagining it even after she told me that I was and that my trepidation was increasing as a result. She only asked me if I wanted another cup of coffee, and further, that she would not sympathize with her clients but that I would get what I deserved. Mr. Paleman explained that scenario to me as an example of the modern treatment of mentally ill persons in this country, and then laughed at the top of his lungs. Then explained that he wasn't laughing because it was sad but was in fact laughing because it was funny. When I then asked him to explain to me in detail what constituted an idea as being humorous or indeed tragic and if there was a formula for such differentiation he became very serious, and apprehensive, and then, out of nowhere, suddenly vanished.

To rig a slot machine for an 8 figure payout a very complicated sequence of events must take place, Mr. Letcher said very seriously the next day. I was told, recently, that I couldn't come close to writing a story but that I must come to a well deserved point. No matter how many circles I went in. If I didn't come to a point, I would; disappear, as one of my captives told me. I was told by these masked men that they had successfully kidnapped and cloned Steven Soderesverg, and then tortured and killed him, for a film he released in 2002, without their permission. He was replaced and the subsequent body of films released under his name were more mature for the American population. Which, was not d-33 classified for the idea of coming and going but still being in one place, and, more importantly, the concept of; not blowing it, which no one in this little country would ever understand except for the person who they had killed whom they told me was their own experiment to begin with the origin of which they had produced in the form of a biological specimen from a code deciphered by a polish scientist in 1954 and which he was told to never even hint at but did and was killed also. Just this evening, I seen that Mr. Holves was, unable, to attend his court hearing and no further explanation was given and when I got back to my cell George C. Scott was standing by the window smiling and he said, there was a war fought in your head, I was there. And further, that we had to get control of the big board immediately. And if you think that I am not the most dangerous and unsound psychopath to have ever walked the planet, Mr.Letcher said, that only means that I am also the greatest con artist to have ever walked the face of the earth. But I'm not conning now nor is there any slickery involved currently. Human beings are not responsible for the environment that formed the way they feel, the way they think, and the way they act. That is what only .08% of the population knows and is the core foundation of social democracy. Free will, moral responsibility, and the idea of the universality of good and evil forces in general is why .08% of the population of this world has 90% of the wealth and the rest believe what those tell them. An adolescent child will believe absolutely anything it is told. Any child, anywhere, at any age, will accept any type of environment and any set of circumstances along with it imaginable. Once the pattern is molded habits will recur incessantly through the lifespan of the organism. It is the height of irrationality to assume that a child born into poverty who witnesses his own mother prostituting, or a child who is physically abused, or a child who is severely malnourished, or a child who is sexually abused, or a child who is abandoned, or a child who is never shown affection, a person who thinks that such a child will later in their life understand the concept of assuming responsibility for their actions needs their prefrontal cortex removed and I would do it happily and would even eat the brain matter of someone who didn't understand what I am writing.

When a massacre takes place it affects the relatives and immediate acquaintances of the victims and 45 days later, is forgotten by 99.92% of the populace. The news media informs this nation of whodoers that it was terrible, it was tragic, it was unfortunate. Other news personnel, titled experts, give their opinions about violence, gun control, and how they wish every last person in the country could be completely safe and out of harm's way and never have to experience a tragedy. Then, the alleged suspects' picture is shown. The news media spokeswoman frowns. He is deemed an enemy of the people, and it is assumed by all that the shooter grew up in a perfectly normal middle class family and was loved and had all of the rights and privileges entitled to anyone else and was in no way shape or form mentally ill but due to the suspects inherent; evilness, I guess, that he was born with, and wasn't taught, or instilled upon by his environment, he up and decided to shoot a hundred people. That is the assumption.

The suspect is years later found guilty in something called trial, Mr.Letcher said. Subsequently given a life sentence. Subsequently placed in solitary confinement, and then given mild generic psychotropics' until he dies and is never even thought of again. But because I have 300 billon neurons in my head, and am also ahead of the curve, I have thought about it and I want you to put all of that down in your book Mr. Letcher told me.

Eventually, a long time after Mr. Letcher died, I was released. I had spent 8 years in complete isolation with no human contact and I was very discomforted by people, moving objects, and tall bright brown, white, and steel buildings. I quickly amassed a fortune from various religious fundraisers and ponzi schemes. I had a brain transplant. For optimal enhancement. I built a small compound in southeast Georgia. In a secure underground complex I rebuilt my isolation cell and locked myself in it for two months to reinduce the situational awareness and repression of short term memory processes it presented me with. I had a time released locked door that I set from the outside so that I couldn't leave when I wanted to. When the timer was up, and I came out for the first time, I can't describe what happened. Anyone within 5 miles of my compound I kidnapped and tortured. I enjoyed a long and intimate conversation with a person before I, disassociated them. I have found no other experience worthwhile, or as equally compelling. Before I went back into the isolation tank I was put under anesthesia by my assistants, and had my brain removed again. It was put into a barrel with prunes and sugar and underwent the fermentation process, then was restored. Days later, it was removed from the barrel, drained, and then put back into my head. Electrodes, a memory disk, and small lithium batteries were also added before it was replaced, as Jisoo Kim told me that this procedure would cure me.

At one point in my life I was an honest person, Mr. Letcher told me. Now, I am a total and absolute liar and can't be trusted. I don't think twice about the truth in any matter and wouldn't care for any truth at all outside of a way that I could slander it. When King Solomon was writing proverbs, and was repeatedly illuminating the difference between wise men and fools, take every last word he wrote on how evil and base men thrive on foolishness and hypocrisy, and I am the sum and final product of all such foolishness. I could write a book for instance, a clear, and mathematically formulated instruction manual on how the planet and the human race could be organized and could thrive efficiently into the future, but wouldn't, for the simple fact that I do not see the benefit over a long period of time in repetitious activity. Instead, like Mr. Nolman, I find chaos and the idea of anarchy neurologically appealing. It tickles me to my core. But someone like Mr. Nolman, who likes to rub it into everyone's' face how clever he is, like Solomon, well, I like to battle with such people. You think in the end people didn't prove how sick they really can be, when the chips got low?

A maniac, who was, clearly, inspired by Mr. Nolmans previous film attempted to wipe out an entire audience full of moviegoers. Then, instead of people who see movies and think about them boycotting the new film, or at least showing some respect to the dead, they poured into theaters in the following days just to egg on the next maniac.

No one, absolutely not even one news channel spokesperson or newspaper columnist has said anything about the second film having truly inspired the neuroscientist.

Ha ha ha ha ha ha ha ha ha. That's so funny. No one has put 5 and 4 together. Most people I talk to, and I've spoken to hundreds on this issue, just think that the fellow did the shooting randomly, or, would have done it anyway with or without inspiration. Lol, lol, lol, lol, lol, lol, lol, lol, lol. This world is the best one I have ever been to. I told the Marquis that I wanted in on a good comedy but I didn't think that it would be this funny. This is too good to be true. Mr. Nolman is so silly. Mr. Letcher told me to shoot myself for vomiting. Ha ha ha ha ha ha ha ha ha. No one knows what I just insinuated. Lol lol lol lol lol lol lol lol lol.

Do you want to know what is sad, Mr. Paleman asked me before he killed himself in my room, on my mattress? I was a good person. I was decent. I could have went happily along with what everyone else was doing. A job. A family with Jisoo Kim. Old age and prosperity, and grandchildren. In the end, I am only a product of my environment, and cannot deviate from a mathematical equation. I am as I have been made. I am not going to take responsibility for anything not even this book. I am a puppet, and am not capable of complex creative self-imagery in any form. A thousand times a day I suddenly, find, myself doing something that I am not, aware of. I have several times caught myself in the very act, of writing this book, with no recollection whatsoever of what drove me to begin writing or, what propelled me to do so. I do not even understand the concept of the process that produces the words that I am writing at this moment. I am not in control. Months on end in complete darkness and without any noise at all gave rise to an over heightened sense of touch. With a wet finger I could pinpoint which parts of my brain were doing what. With a piece of feces I drew a map over these various brain regions. Which led to the ability to actually feel large strands of neurons reacting to various stimulants.

In the isolation cell I carried my brain around in my hands for years. I was told that it contained dark matter, and therefore could potentially have negative or quantum properties. I threw it against the wall a thousand times. I slammed it on the ground, I stepped on it, I stomped it, I held it down and fornicated it and then I tried to flush it down the toilet but it wouldn't go. I licked it, I chewed on it, I played with it, I threw it up into the air as one might toss an apple up into the air before they grab it and take a bite out of it. I took apart the 4 lobes and juggled them. In the end, I ate my own brain. Only a small percentage of the population knows that if you run your left index finger around the top of your head 7 times while repeating I'm slightly ahead of the curve, you can gently and without any pain at all lift up the top of your skull like a toilet seat lid. And then, if you're careful, you can pull your brain out, which, can be exchanged with someone else who knows the same trick.

Heath Letcher said that there were some things he just couldn't tell me. I asked him if it was because he thought I might spill the beans? I wouldn't spill the beans he said, but, if I wanted to put it that way, I was a bucket that wouldn't hold water. Mr. Paleman quickly countered his argument by saying that if I was a bucket, I wouldn't leak but that I would spill. Mr. Paleman then also became furious once again, for no reason at all, and told Mr. Letcher and I that we were so out of touch with reality that we needed a talk show. But, no one would listen I told him. Then we will talk to the aliens Mr. Letcher said.

At one point, I had 3 runts running around in circles in my isolation cell. They would run by me, and around each other cussing and yelling the entire way and sometimes pinching my butt as they ran by. They wore hooded robes so that I wouldn't have to look at them, and for it, they passed gas incessantly. Then, one day as I was peeling potatoes I told Mr. Letcher that I felt like I was in a Van Gogh painting. You're more like van gone he replied. At which point, I actually woke up, underneath a bridge, with a large sackel full of dynamite strapped around my shoulder. You're a bridgeblower Mr. Skinningway told me. Not a thinker. Don't go mixing too many things together, which is what you have done here. I carried Stephen Crane around on my shoulders and we spent years together in brothels all over Europe and southeast Asia. Women, men, transsexuals, animals, cafes in Paris, casinos, opium, liquor, and murder. Miss Rooney was with us also. She was the first women in Europe to have a tattoo put on her face. But, as Fitzgerald, if he were here, I am sure, would agree with me if I said, there is no cure, that is without side effects. I am not an actor, Mr. Letcher told me, but it would have been an honor, if I was still alive, honestly, to have starred in a film version of Tender Is The Night with Mara Rooney. And you know who I would be, and you know who she would be. Although, by the end of the film I wouldn't have to act, but she would, he said, and then smiled.

Mr. Paleman told Mr. Letcher and I that we ought to be ashamed of all the things we know and then, the way we disgrace all of it. Mr. Letcher then finally lunged out at Mr. Paleman, forgetting all self-restraint, and beat him severely before he was pulled away and subdued. I'm showing off my level of intelligence in the most disgusting manner ever conceived I told Mr. Paleman as he was being carted off. Never in the history of the world has someone in such a lowly place ever, ever, imagined themselves to be on a pedestal with the greatest in the world, and yet, here I am doing it. Then I laughed at myself until I fell and hit my head on the toilet.

Do you know what they use to call me before I took my brain out of my head and swapped it with Mr. Nolmans?

2 days ago I was transferred to a new state hospital. I left behind my old friends, and my old personality. This person, the one you are dealing with now, cannot remember the past. I can only remember the past for one day. That is why I have covered my body with tattoos.

This person that I am going to tell you about is one of the greatest individuals that I have ever met. He was born on January the 5th, 1972, in southeast Georgia. He was the only son of a pecan farmer, as his mother died in childbirth. His father's name was James Leroy Williams. A devout Christian and Alcoholic. My cellmates name is James Leroy Williams Jr. We shall simply call him Leroi though, out of nostalgia.

My writing is a fetish, as you can see. It is an orgy involving my brain and the souls of dead writers. The only difference between this person and the last one, is that, I would rather someone, that is similar to myself, would share his or her views artistically rather than acting out on them. Just look at Francisco De Goya, the finest example of subtlety. I am by no means a fan of Gus Van Sant, but he did make one film titled Elephant, that probably no more than 50 people have watched with aesthetic pleasure. The last person you were reading on the other hand, was one cup of coffee away from an act of arson or several murders. That is what I was told, it was a theory. I was transferred, almost with fluency, and I have been put on a new medication. I have spent 3 days alone in my new isolation cell with James Williams Jr. My psychosis, like everything else on this planet, is just warming up. Innocent people do not know better. No one knows what they are dealing with. This is the first concept of the psychological aesthetics of Murder. This new person, urges young observant individuals to make an opening statement in an acceptable manner. One that will gain them lasting notoriety and wealth and, or, a cure for their mental illness, which can be bought. If that doesn't work, if the urge is still too strong, join the military. Or, go to a country where there is a civil war or revolution and join the rebels. Leroi is a biblical scholar. He memorized the book of proverbs, and he told me, therein lies wisdom. As a child he strolled endlessly through fields of pecan trees. His father took him to church every Sunday, but for that, he rarely ever seen his father. Instead, he was raised by a young black maid. Who fed him, bathed him, clothed him, taught him and nurtured him in every manner conceivable and whom he later married. Until the age of 13, Leroi told me, as far as he knew it, he was a good person, and was passionate about his life, his father, and what he knew about the world in general. Then one day, out of the blue, all of that changed.

It was during the spring of 1983. In the early evening just as the sun was setting. Leroi had been strolling along between two rows of pecan trees when he came upon a large stone wall. Written on the wall, where he approached, were the words; Personality Decay

Theory. He jumped over it. Whereupon he discovered, miles and miles of cages, made of sectioned off galvanized fencing. He walked along in amazement. There were people, actual people, in the cages. There were also dogs, chickens, cows, pigs, peacocks, horses, raccoons, beavers, and a cage with an alligator in it. After walking along some ways Leroi came upon his father who was hosing out a cage that had two young women in it and when his father seen him, he said, one day, this will all be yours. This new isolation cell I am in is well-lit. Light bulbs, and a window. I have been here for 3 days and I haven't had a cell mate for the last two years. For 60 days I had nothing, no psychiatrists, no medicine, no kidnappers, nothing. Now, I am in an isolation cell with Leroi Jones. I am sitting in my bunk behind a set of steel bars which are three feet from a caged wall, which is 6 feet from a Plexiglas wall, which is 4 feet from a concrete block wall, which is 275 feet from a galvanized fence topped with razor wire, which is 15 feet from a 20 foot high galvanized fence reinforced with chicken wire and razor wire the whole way up and which also has an electrical current running through it. That is what separates me from the world as of January the 5th 2013. I have lost my mind 21,212 times in the last three days and this book is the product of someone who hates me yet is inside of my head. I am 29 years old and have spent most of my life in state institutions. If you have never been to one, and spent some time there, it is a bad idea to commit yourself to a state prison or hospital for the rest of your life if you are only 17 to 26 years old. Even if no one cares about you, isolation with no external stimulation at all will absolutely horrify you far more than the world you already know. There are some painful experiences that produce enlightenment, others more severe that do not.

There is no explanation, for instance, for how often I wake up and realize that I am in a pitch black padded room and the water is still running in the sink. This person, the one writing now, you only think is your friend. 29 years ago I found a way inside your head and hid there and every time you dream I am alive and well and am digging deeper and am burrowing myself in further. Along the way, whatever I find I kill and eat and I have been doing that for 125,000 years. I always knew that I came out of a pitch black cave, but had to be assured of it once again. I use to put my hand on the wall or draw the animals I killed on the wall with my own blood, but now I do this instead. Herzog.

Which did you cut first, your neck, or your wrist? Mara Rooney asked me that after I had sacrificed my twenties, my thirties, my career, and my mental health for her happiness. I cut my wrists because I wanted to get it over with, when it didn't happen quickly enough, that's when I cut my neck. You should have just shot yourself she said. I wanted the complete experience I told her, I wanted to feel it. You're lying, she said despicably. I have been two people I told her. Who had shot themselves in the head and survived. One of them used an SKS underneath his chin. The other one used a 45 caliber underneath his chin. Then you should have put the gun inside your mouth idiot, she said and then laughed. At which point, after thinking about it for several seconds, I asked her, is that what you really want? To which, she rolled her eyes, and stated, I'm like most women, I don't want a boyfriend, or a companion, or anyone else thinking that they are equal to me, I want someone who is going to worship me, go write about that.

But, that is how I think as well. I do not like the concept of equality with other people. The pyramids didn't build themselves did they, Miss Rooney even asked me. Of course they didn't I told her. This is a pyramid. There is a birds head above my shoulders. 9 years after I woke up in the facility they made me in they removed my head. They said that they were going to put an electrode deep inside of my brain and that it would cure me. This was all part of a new government program. The head of an IBIS that had been cultured with human stem cells was surgically implanted above my 33rd spinal column. 70 years from now I will bend time and go back to Egypt once again, will they will worship me and I will teach them how to paint hieroglyphs. For now, I use my old skull as a beggar's cup. I'd even almost bet, that the Russians will take me in. 10 years from now, when everyone will have caught wind of me, you haven't yet read what is to follow, and everyone will be screaming to the top of their lungs for my blood, the Russians will hide me away somewhere and treat me as a long lost son and I'll save my darkest secrets for the books that I'll write for them. I'll outdo even Dostoevsky and Gogol. I am Russian, when I'm reading, though I'm English, and a direct descendant from the first well-known serial killer of the religious era, but, I'd trade it all to have been born in St. Petersburg, and I'd trade that for a pecan orchard, a hundred acres of cotton fields and 50 servants in southeast Georgia. My skin is as pale as a white rose petal, a shade paler than even old saint squat, and blood, can only be seen in my cheeks and in my hair. Yet I would shave my head to renounce wisdom, and wear a birds mask to hide two sides of a face that no one sees anyway, if someone could perform an operation that would make me forget my past. To have a city inside your head, and allow it, as I do, is the true definition of unselfishness.

Mara Rooney just read what I wrote, I am sure of it, and then, she looked at me for a very long time before she said, you are the absolutely most treacherous and inhumane person who has ever scrambled about, in fact, you are so disgusting, that no one should ever consider killing you, but instead, everywhere you go people ought to point at you and laugh as absurdly as they possibly can and then, they ought to spit on you, hit you, kick you, and take whatever you have on top of that. You should only be allowed to eat out of dumpsters, and bums themselves ought to turn their chins up at you in disgrace and that is only the beginning. But I love you, I told her, and I want to have a family with you, and I would do anything for you if, just once a week, you would read poetry to me for an hour.

To which, she opened her mouth up wide in shock, as if I had greatly insulted her. But then, once she remembered who I was she composed herself and simply said; never in your wildest dreams.

Yesterday I told Jisoo Kim about the analogies Mr. Letcher and Mr. Paleman had made about this person being a bucket that wouldn't hold water on the one hand, and a bucket that would spill on the other. Personally, she said, I reminded her of a metal bucket full of leaches she had seen once in China.

There are two birds, my new psychiatrist began telling me, the phrase to which he was presenting me with, was a riddle.

I already know this one, I interrupted him. The first bird Noah sent out, the Raven, was the April fools bird.

He then stared at me for several seconds.

He was sitting with his legs crossed at the knees and had a pad in his lap upon which he was making notes about this person.

What types of medication have you been on in the past and what are you taking currently?

Seriquil, Wellbutren, topomaxx, thorozene and rimrods, recently they switched me over to respirol and sylexcia, and another one.

How do you feel right now, he asked me. Are you feeling anxious or depressed? Are you hearing voices? At this moment, do you feel like doing harm to yourself or others?

Yes sir.

Yes sir to what, he asked me.

To all of it.

How many voices are you hearing right this moment?

One.

Is it a voice that you hear often?

No sir, only occasionally.

What is it saying exactly?

Since right after lunch yesterday, I suppose you could say that he's been telling me a story he wants me to write. Now and again on the other hand, he comments about current events as well, some things seemingly arbitrary though. I can tell you that he does not like you at all, he just told me that if it wasn't for this strait jacket he would kill you himself.

That's flattering, the psychiatrist said. What is the story about?

A serial killer being held in a secret government facility that is being experimented on.

Do you or have you ever experienced any hallucinations?

Yes sir.

On a scale of 1-10, with 1 being seldom and 10 being almost constantly, how often do you have hallucinations?

10.

What color is your strait jacket he then asked me?

Lime green.

I am going to say 3 words and in a few minutes I am going to want you to say them back to me. Chair, and then he pointed to an empty chair. Fan, then he pointed to a fan on his desk. Lightbulb, and then he pointed to the light fixture above us. Have you ever been abused, including up to your current stay at this institution?

I have.

How many times would you say you have been abused and again I would like for you to use the scale I described to you earlier of 1-10.

10.

It appears that your face is slightly lacerated, do you have any other bruises or injuries that you are aware of?

No sir.

He then made notes and almost an entire minute passed by before he looked up at me and asked the next question. Do you think your current medication is helping you or would you like to try something different?

I would like to be put back on the thorozene, and the wellbutrens, sir.

Did you grow up with your father, your mother or both?

Neither sir.

With whom?

With an aunt.

Did she abuse you?

Yes sir.

Physically or sexually?

Both.

Did she have a husband or children of her own?

No husband, but she did have 3 children sir.

Boys or girls?

2 boys and one girl.

Were they older or younger than you?

Older sir.

What was your relationship like with these older children and again I would like for you to use the scale of 1-10, 1 this time being a very poor and abusive relationship and with 10 being a positive and loving relationship.

1.

I am going to give you a writing tablet. He reached over and opened one of his desk drawers and pulled out a new yellow writing pad. Writing can be therapeutic and helpful he added as he shoved the writing pad down between the folds of my strait jacket. Then from his top desk drawer he pulled out 2 small flexible pens, and placed them down between my arms also. When the guards take you back to your cell they are going to remove that strait jacket and this evening you will be given the thorozene you requested. We do not have wellbutren at this facility but we do have a new SSRI that we can try you out on to see if it helps you. We also have a new program here. . . . . . . that might help you as well. If you begin documenting these sessions and whatever other experiences you have while you are here at this institution eventually you can have certain privileges that have been taken away from you restored. Would you like the opportunity to be around other inmates again? It would take time, but with your cooperation with the mental health staff and the correctional officers at this institution, it could one day become a possibility.

Yes sir.

What were the three words I asked you to remember?

I had to think, I had forgotten. I began to turn the previous events over, and around, and to follow the paths of the astrocytes, as the psychiatrist told me; that was what was happening, and then, when I looked over I remembered the empty chair.

Then I seen the fan. There was something else, but I couldn't remember it. I looked around. To my left, then to my right. The psychiatrist was just staring at me. During the entire session he stared at my eyes and never looked away from then.

You don't remember the 3rd item?

No sir.

What color is your strait jacket?

Lime green sir.

Do you remember the number you gave me for the second question I asked you in which I wanted a number for a response?

10.

But you do not recall the 3rd item I told you to remember?

I thought long and hard about it. But I couldn't remember. No sir.

Look up.

When I looked up I immediately remembered the light fixture.

Light fixture sir.

Not exactly, but that's close.

So I looked again, and I thought about it, I am sure, in multiple varieties of insinuation, but I came to nothing.

Light bulb the psychiatrist finally said. There are two light bulbs in the light fixture above you that are about 4 feet long and 2 to 3 inches in diameter.

When I looked back up, I didn't see them. There was just an empty light fixture. There were in fact 2 fixtures on each side, but no light bulbs.

No sir. I do not see the lightbulbs.

The psychiatrist then made notes.

Do you see any other light fixtures in this room, except for the one above you. You can stand up and look around if you would like.

I stood up, and swept the room with my eyes, but I didn't see any other fixtures.

No sir, I do not see any.

Sit back down please.

He then reached over and picked up a large book off of his desk. What is this, he asked me.

It is a book.

What does it say on the spine? Then he turned it sideways so I could see the spine of the book perpendicularly.

D, S, M, 5, I said.

That's correct.

Now let me ask you, how is it that you think you have just now looked at this book, and read the title, without their being light bulbs in the fixture above you. Seeing as how there are no windows in this room, no other light fixtures, and no other source of light.

I don't know.

Take a look again and tell me if you still don't see them.

So I looked again. But still I didn't see any lightbulbs.

What were the names of your three cousins?

Alex, Pete and Georgie.

That is all for today. I will see you again next Thursday.

But I didn't know when that would be, as I didn't know what day of the week it was yesterday.

I was then escorted back to my cell by 3 officers. They removed the strait jacket then set the pad and the two pens down on top of my mattress. 2 of them were standing in front of me and one in the doorway. I was suddenly knocked down to the ground and kicked repeatedly for about ten seconds. Then they left and slammed the door shut behind me.

There is a Plexiglas window in this cell, it has a metal plate covering most of it from the outside but there is a one inch slit running down the side through which I can look out and see the sky. Which is red right now.

I was beaten and kicked by the guards yesterday I explained to my new psychiatrist.

He made notes, but said nothing.

What are you going to do about it I asked him?

I will make an inquiry, he said plainly.

I apologize sir, and I don't mean to sound rude, but you seem completely unaffected by what I just told you. It almost seems as if, you don't really care.

Well, I treat all allegations of abuse at this institution that are reported to me by my patients seriously. But, this is a mental health institution and more often than not inmates make false or exaggerated allegations.

It was the 3 guards that escorted me back to my cell after our first meeting, I told him.

He just continued to stare me.

Would you like to talk about the reason why you are currently at this institution?

Do you mean the immediate reason , or the underlying reasons, I asked him?

Were you in the military?

Yes sir.

Did you or did you not open fire on a group of people standing outside of an art gallery with a government issued weapon?

At which point, I must admit that I no longer felt like I could trust the psychiatrist, or that he held my therapy as a priority. So I didn't say anything else. We were both quiet for several minutes. I had forgotten about the incident. I do not think that he should have brought it up. How many years had I been gone? The number 342 passed before my eyes. What does that number mean? Even now I can't remember.

Before I knew it I was on top of the psychiatrist. He was agile, and was not submissive, but in a matter of seconds I had him in a rear naked choke hold, and killed him.

NO HUMAN CONTACT

For the last few days I have been reading several newspapers and magazines. As you can very well assume, previously I hadn't done so in at least 26 months. I was reminded, of the characteristic traits, entailing human social interaction. Particularly, how information is most commonly conveyed. For example, plainly, and directly. I know that I am not doing a very good job of that. I apologize. To start at the beginning, in my childhood, the reason why I cannot narrate a memoir along a consistent timeline, is because by modern standards in book writing, or article writing, the subject content that I have to present, for instance; there have been no studies on the symptoms of accumulative instant-ness syndrome from prolonged isolation, would simply be unacceptable. This subject matter could be read but would not be beneficial to anyone, and more importantly, people would not feel comfortable around me in the future.

As to my future I do not have one. I am in an institution. I am not allowed to say which one. Whether or not anything I write will ever attain any monetary value would not affect my standard of living as it could for any other journalist or writer. The only topic I have to discuss is my immediate environment and the various stories that I have heard from other mentally ill inmates. And, whatever I have accumulated out of the newspapers that are occasionally made available, and, what I see on the news. That is the extent of my individual personality. Which I know is not unique, or separate.

I have spent most of my life in these institutions. I did not complete high school. I did not go to college. The reason why I am reiterating that is because, like my cohorts in this institution, I have no interest in the government of this country. None whatsoever. Healthcare reform, the fiscal cliff, government spending, global warming, the unemployment rate, the decline of religious belief, articles of that nature are passed over by my eyes faster than the advertisements for hotel quality pillows. If there is an article on a 15 year old who has killed his entire family with an Assault rifle I am suddenly interested. I am mentally ill and find such articles fascinating and more along the lines of my living environment. 88 people dead in a middle eastern country due to three separate suicide bombings in one day, I thrive off of such information. I read, and then reread the details. I fixate on the pictures for hours. I take ahold of them in my mind. I dwell on them. I lay inside of them. I ponder their meaning. I reenact them thousands of times throughout the night as I lay stiff as a corpse.

With patience, you are going to watch me take all of this, and stretch it. The more it's stretched, the better. There are elements that are currently bundled together, but, when pulled apart, individually give much more significant explanations into the concepts of suicide and murder, and the psychobiological processes that lead up to such events.

I just lied. I am so good at lying. It is my fetish to be false.

I have been so false. I won't say where I have been. There is no telling where. I have been a coward and have been displaying my petty imagination all along. I am a coward and am not worthy of anyone's affection, or trust, and wouldn't want either even if they could be had. I am disgusting and am not sorry for it. I don't even trust myself. The reason why I write, the real reason, is because I don't have the courage to talk to people, and, because when I do say something, I don't like to be interrupted, and I don't like to hear other people's opinions. People are fools. Around other people I feel precocious, and ashamed, because of my intelligence. I don't even know where to look when I'm around people. Most people, are happy just to get away from me as soon as they can.

I have a physical disease that I won't bother naming. I do have one, I'm not lying about that. As to whether I am mentally ill, which I have claimed, I do not think that can be determined. I have been told conflicting variations of what is wrong with me by several dozens of people who either hate me or do not care for me. When I was released, and knew that I was dying and had less than a year left to live, I obsessed over only one very clear idea. Redemption. I was deadest on randomly killing someone and getting away with it. That first murder would be the beginning of my revenge towards a world that had made me, and wasn't ashamed to do so. I couldn't tolerate myself as being just a bystander, even from the beginning.

I received a check from the government when they let me out and with it I rented a cheap hotel room and didn't come out for a week. For 8 years I hadn't seen a television and so for days I laid in bed glued to one. The very first show that I watched had a group of scientists sitting in a circle around a fish tank and underneath it was an earthquake simulator and the scientists were watching to see what the fish would do.

A week later I walked over to a store for the first time. I was eyeballed by everyone in it. My head throbbed the entire time and I felt dizzy. To be around other people again, without restraints, produced a surge of endorphins. On the way back to my room I caught sight of a blond haired woman coming out of another room about 7 rooms down from mine.

Mein Zimmer.

She had on cheap worn out black stockings, a black skirt, a small white t-shirt, altogether she was very trashy looking and when she seen me, the dumb look on her face didn't change but she stopped and just stared at me. When I got to my door I made a weak gesture with my hand motioning her to come in and she came straight on without any hesitation.

Instantly I decided to kill her. I gave her 50 dollars, which she asked for, and I then began wondering how I could kill her without her screaming, or making any noticeable amount of sound. My loathing and self-contempt, I noticed, had momentarily subsided, and I stood in amazement of the situation. No one had seen her come in, no one anywhere in the world would know she had been with me, if it went well, I could get away with it legitimately.

She took her clothes off. I hadn't been in the presence of a naked woman in so many years, it obviously had an effect on me. I sodomized her, she was oblivious to it, but after only a minute or so I slowly wrapped my arm around her neck, and began choking her.

For a fleeting moment she reached back and made an attempt to claw at my eyes. I exerted so much pressure on her neck that she instead grabbed at my arm and tried to free herself but, to no avail. Once she was dead, I finished sodomizing her and then I carried her into the bathroom and dropped her in the tub. I stood over her and marveled. It had all happened so quickly. It was so easy. What did I feel? It felt like the first time I had slept in a coffin. It felt translucent. I had succeeded. I laid down in the bed and slept for hours.

When I woke up, I had the urge to sit her up in a chair and talk to her. When I went to pick her up though, as I thought about just laying her over the edge of the bathtub, she was as stiff as a board. I should have known, I knew, but I had forgotten how quickly the process happened. I then left the hotel and caught a city bus over to a large supercenter. I purchased luggage, trash bags, bleach, plastic gloves, washrags, towels, and also 100 dollars' worth of groceries so that I wouldn't appear conspicuous. Once I was outside of the store I put all of the items in the largest piece of luggage, put the groceries in the dumpster behind the building, and then went back to the bus stop.

The first piece of luggage would have been just large enough for the small body but instead I cut her up into sections. I cut off her head and her hands first, and put them into one bag. Then I cut off her legs and her arms and put them into another, and her torso I put into the largest piece of luggage.

I poured pounds of raw coffee beans in with the various parts and wrapped each group of parts into 4 trash bags, and then, covered them completely in duct tape. I left the hotel again and walked a half of a mile to a storage unit complex I had seen and rented a storage space for one year. Instead of wasting time trying to find a place to bury the pieces of luggage, I calculated that I would just put them into a storage unit where they wouldn't be thought about until long after I was dead and gone myself. I had a taxi cab take me and the luggage over to the unit, and then I went back to the hotel. Watched movies, read the newspaper, and drank strong cups of coffee for several days.

I never talk to people and so I want you to feel privileged for this little conversation of ours. That is what this individual told me. It was in that hotel room that I seen a film that changed something inside of me. You have mentioned psychosis, and have hinted that it has to be triggered. I never would have killed anyone, I am sure of it, or would have had the notion in my head that I had to do so, until I seen a film called the   . It was on television early on a Saturday morning, at about 4 a.m. Things have lingered in my mind, as you can imagine, concepts that were like shadows. Particularly, I shouldn't be telling you this, but I cried while I watched it. The final 3 minutes of that film shook me to my core. From then, until now, I have thought about it often, and the formula involving it. Its environment. Its interaction with people who have seen it. The entire history of film would have to be studied, reviewed, broken down statistically, and looked at, rationally, finally diagnosed, to understand precisely how grotesque and out of place some films are in this world. But all of those charts, and research studies aside; I want you to ask yourself this question: what is the purpose of a film?

What is supposed to happen? What is the object? What final product is intended, he stated with much emphasis.

Think rationally. As a rule, how do human beings learn?

By imitation? By mimicking behavior?

2500 years after Aristophanes, and 2000 years after Plutarch, film, and storytelling have reached very highly intangible levels, not only emotionally perplexing, but neurologically destabilizing. The pretext has become a ghastly comparison to the actual sacrifice of the illusion.

So my real question to you, sir, since you think yourself benign to present a film upon the subject of sacrifice. What is the point in making a film such as The P   . Here's a better question, you see what type of a person I am, what do you want someone like myself to do after I see that film? Which behavioral scene of that film would you like me to imitate? All along did you simply wish for me to quit my day job, and commit myself to a new life long journey of studying magic tricks, and deceiving people including my family? Even better, even better than all of that, which emotional excerpt of that film would you like for me to convey to the people I come into contact with? Are any two people in that film on an even keel with one another?

Since you are writing a book, or claim that you are, make sure you ask Mr. Nolman, outright, personally, why all of the reoccurring themes of instability, disfigurement, and suicide?

Then he asked me; is it pathetic that a person of my lowly mental capability should be so obsessed with Mr. Nolman? Well, I told him,

Plato had Aristophanes Clouds buried underneath his pillow, Truman Capote had an upscale retail store that he idolized, as a concept foundation for a well written story, and I have Mr. Nolman.

I thought about it for several months, and I ended up cutting off the pinky finger on my right hand late on a Sunday night. You are better than Robert Louis Stevenson, Mr. Letcher told me, you are living the real dream. No wife, no kids, no friends, no coffee shops and 5 star restaurants, no traveling around and seeing the world, just one city, and living in the poorest area. Living amongst the trash and not taking any psychotropics. Not talking to anyone. Not shaving. Only brushing my teeth occasionally. Wearing the same clothes for days on end. Going out and killing people on the sly. Collecting odds and ends. Amassing a library. Cutting out certain newspaper articles and laminating them to the walls of my apartment. Reading about the homicide detectives trying to catch me, and, in short, living the life of a real psychopath. The song, and the dance. And writing about it.

I have schizophrenia, a fellow told me yesterday.

What kind of schizophrenia, I asked him?

Just the regular kind.

He had been gone for several days. They took him away, and then, 3 days later, he was back in this unit.

I went to Q dorm. I wanted to get put back on my medication, he told me.

What medication, specifically, I asked him.

There's 3. Respirol, another pill for the side effects of the respirol, and dee, and then he couldn't remember the entire name of the third one.

What kind of side effects does the respirol give you?

It makes my arms stiff.

What is the third pill for?

It's a mood stabilizer.

A diazapam?

No.

Some type of ssri?

He didn't respond then, but he was rubbing his chin, I guessed, wondering himself.

To look at this fellow, and to watch him for say, 2 minutes, you automatically knew that you were dealing with someone who was not at all well. For one thing, his eyes were sunken into his skull, as if he were predisposed towards sulking and despair. Then, when asked why he was at the institution. . . . . . . stalking. Aggravated stalking actually, he said very naturally, then, looking out at me skeptically he added, it's true too.

We were from the same city, this fellow and I, and with this connection laid between us, he volunteered that there was really nothing wrong with him but that, he lied to the psychiatrists just to get put on the medication.

Why would you want to take respirol if there's nothing wrong with you, I asked him?

I like the way it makes me feel. It makes me feel tired.

So you're not schizophrenic I asked him again plainly.

No, I just use to take a lot of Lysergic acid and other drugs and I feel like I need something to help me come down off of it. Do you know what Lysergic acid does he then asked me?

I shook my head.

It increases glutamate release in the cerebral cortex and is the only substance on the planet thought to do so.

I was then called by another person 50 feet away to come and get something and so I left that individual where he was sitting.

When I came back, he shot me a momentary glance, sideways, that made me shudder. It was a murderous look, and he stroked his Adams apple before he turned his head away.

You are a very, spurious, person he told me. You have been sheltered and are basically useless. 50-100 years from now, potentially 150 years from now, but I think much sooner, robots will be replacing the essential needs of cheap labor and the majority of the otiose human race, yourself included, will be eliminated. I think the population could be reduced by as much as 600 percent by the year 2090, if the essential personnel are able to take control.

Why would you say something like that, I asked him in a very low tone of voice, so as not to provoke him. What is the point in telling someone that, even if it were true?

Because I have no control over, let's say, 80 percent of my behavioral responses. Every now and then, I am myself, in a way, and am allowed to operate within a set of guidelines. But most of the time, I am locked away, and can only wonder about my non adaptive behaviors after they have occurred. I am infected with toxoplasma gondii. It is a parasite that dictates the majority of my behavior. It causes me to take a high number of risks, including what I just said, and even to engage in criminal activity which is why I ended up at this institution.

What is the name of the parasite?

Toxoplasma gondii.

Would you spell it for me?

He did, he spelled it out and I wrote it down at the top of this page.

And you expect me to believe that this parasite controls your behavior, including the things you say.

Once again I will remind you that you are a very naive person, and if it wasn't for the fact that I cannot control myself, I wouldn't even be talking to you.

Everyone was quiet after it happened. I was cuffed and taken away. When we arrived at the place that they took me to, there were 4 masked men waiting outside of a large steel building. They took me in and carried me down a long hallway into a large room where they placed me in a chair and strapped me into it motionless. They left and closed the door behind them. I sat there for a long time, wondering what was happening. The events of that morning were running through my head again, and again, and then the door opened and an olive skinned man in a white laboratory coat, with a surgical mask covering his lower face, rolling a cart into the room.

You're not going to enjoy this, but I am, he told me. I'd like to thank you for the opportunity in advance. He produced a scalpel, and immediately, without any warning, stabbed me with it. He slammed it down right above my knee cap and I screamed out at the top of my lungs. He stared at me as he did it. He held the scalpel in place and stared at me. It excited him. He pulled it out and laid it back down on the cart.

We will let it bleed for a while, he said, then he left the room.

I thought I was going to die. My leg was bleeding severely. A few minutes later, he returned with a small cutting torch. In a brush like manner, he painted the small wound with the flame and I remember my own screams then clearly. When he finished, he said,

I am about to give you an injection then I will unstrap you and show you to your room. It is a dark room and there won't be any light at all. There is a toilet and a sink. I am not going to tell you how long you will be in this room but it will be for a very long period of time. Who you are now, you will not be when you leave this facility. Concepts and ideas present now will abandon you. The sequence of events as objects that have been your life, you will despise for what they are going to torture you with.

You will thank me though, once I am through with you. Then he injected me with a syringe full of blue liquid fiction and other poems.

So when was it that you began realizing that you did not have any control over yourself, Jisoo Kim asked me.

When I would realize that I was still in that isolation cell. I thought that I had actually left it a hundred times, and that I had been let out of prison and had started a new life. But then, all of a sudden, I would realize that I was inside of that black room once again, and it would take several minutes, but then, I would hear the watering running. I knew that I was only imagining that I had left, but I wondered what it was that brought me back? How could my mind create the impression that I was gone so realistically, so vividly, and then not continue to live in that delusion indefinitely?

Then what would happen she asked me.

It would take hours, perhaps days, to slip off again, and, I would be gone, but eventually I would come back. It was in those cycles of coming and going, that I slowly realized I had no control over the process itself. I couldn't, make, myself go, or, comeback, and that idea tormented me more than anything else.

So how do you know that you are not in that cell right now? How do you know for sure that you are not still in that room right this very moment? This instant.

That is easy to explain. I only met you a few months ago. I don't remember you from my past. So there is no way I could have just constructed an image of a person as beautiful as you are out of nothing, without a memory of you in my head to build from.

But, she then just stared at me blankly.

What's wrong I asked her?

I'm tired, and we keep going back to this same incident over and over again.

What do you mean, I asked her, and I started to feel nervous again, as if something were wrong all of a sudden. Something very wrong

How is it that you don't ever remember our first date, and then she shifted her hair and sat up straighter, until I ask you if you have looked in the mirror lately?

My hands, and then my feet began tingling.

You've been thinking about it so much, that now I am going to have to start letting you back into your room even slower, and by ruining the end of your dream right before you wake back up. Nor can I tell you how long it will be before you see me again.

There is a very beautiful woman with a Ouija board tattooed on her arm somewhere in Atlanta. If she reads this she will know who I am, and I need you to find me.

I was in Q dorm, with Heath Letcher, all over again. He told me that he wanted me to start over from the beginning, and to tell the truth about everything, without being deceptive.

After all, we live in a free society, he explained to me. And given the freedom you have, literally, to explore the extremes of literary devices, let's push the envelope, shall we. I tried to blow up a boat you see, and failed, but, I did blow up a hospital, and I robbed a few banks and killed a lot of people, and had a good time while I was at it. He smiled widely. As long as I can inspire people like you, and as long as no one with a real brain in their head studies abnormal psychology, or psychopathology, or theories on human learning, or gives two thoughts to the billons of factors that contribute to the make-up of a person, well, I'll continue to have a wonderful time in your head, and so shall you.

At the time I was considered a psych 1, by the department of corrections. Psych 1 being the highest of 3 degrees of severity in terms of maladaptive behavior and mental disorders. My own comorbidity is probably, I am sure, much too complex for me to describe to you, and so I won't bother you with a technical description. I am currently studying an abnormal psychology textbook, because I want to try to understand what is wrong with me, but I will admit that; I am aware of the textbook both depressing me, and causing me to be anxious, as it continues to reveal to me how disadvantaged and inadequate my sociocultural environment was, just to begin with. I have actually read multiple psychology textbooks and volumes of psychoanalytical doctrines and as of this moment all I can ascertain is that there is no hope for me at all.

What has been written about the people who study neuroanatomy, neurochemistry, and abnormal psychology, Mr. Letcher asked me? What leads a person to study such fields of science to begin with? If these are the causes and risk factors for abnormal behavior, and then he read them off as from a list; my diathesis stress model, neurotransmitter imbalances, genetic vulnerabilities, early deprivation or trauma, maladaptive peer relationships, pathogenic societal influences(the influence in this case study being abnormal films), poor genotype environment correlation-poor phenotype correlation. That is a fistful out of a thousand and yet, they will find Mr. Holves guilty and say that he was inherently evil in and of his own will and was completely responsible for his own actions. Even though before he opened fire he yelled out that I am the joker.

At worst, someone will kill you for what you are about to write, but you have to die at some point anyway, and given the necessary, sufficient, and contributory causes of your P.T.S.D. and other disorders, you don't have much time left to live anyway, according to the textbooks. So go on and write about killing a bunch of people, everyone else is doing it, they are killing people all over the world right this very minute. You can also get away with writing what you are about to, because you can tell them that I told you to say it, which I did. You can also label this as fiction or entertainment and get away with it cleanly as well, even if it is what you are really thinking. Also, you can say, well, there are copies of Justine and juliette in American book stores. And Thomas de Quincy and Anthony Burgess for God sakes, if there even is a God, which is starting to look less and less likely. Surely you can write about whatever you want and that's final. After all you're mentally ill and don't know any better.

How Mr. Letcher spewed all of that out I'll never know. He is right here in Q dorm with me, in 2013 at   correctional institute. Psychobiological development, who in the entire world knows what that really means, Mr. Letcher asked me, and then he laughed. Most definitely not a judge, or a district attorney, in the state of Colorado.

A couple of people in the northeastern united states? And then he laughed again. A handful of people in Germany? A mouthful in Switzerland? Then he laughed some more. 50 people, maybe, know what psychobiological development entails, or, know what a pathogenic societal influence is, and then, you have 7 billon twirling, prancing, dancing, religious fanatics and pleasure seekers. Then Mr. Letcher fell on the floor and began laughing so hard he had to hold on to his stomach. 50 people and 7 billon adolescents to pamper who believe whatever they are told during their childhood. He laughed and laughed and laughed, and he was laughing so loud that it hurt my ears and I had to restrain him.

Take all of your bidirectional influences, he told me as I had my hands around his neck, and it will never help 7 billon selfish and undeserving little rabbits understand why James Holves tried to take out a theater full of them.

They claim to be Christians for one, and then he laughed and I had to squeeze down on his throat to quiet him. And two, their stupidity and hatefulness increases with every new attack, and then he just stared at me after he said that.

You're cute, he told me when I finally let him up and he readjusted himself in his purple jacket. You are real cute for what you just did.

Perhaps, what I am doing now, is a self-defense mechanism against my own perspective, Mr. Letcher wrote on the wall above the door in our cell. I am dead, you see, I already killed myself and yet, you go on persisting that I am right here with you at this institution. You are imagining me, and whether I really am here beside you, as a hallucination, or whether I am your attempt at self-full-fillment, the um; dehumanizing mass of society will never understand your perspective. They are in the here and now, and then he rolled his tongue around his lips like he did in the movie. And you're up there. Then he looked up at the ceiling. You're up there with Alfred Jarry and about 40 other people.

Every possible history, he whispered and then he nodded his head. Then he patted me on my knee, and continued nodding his head slowly and repeated quietly; every possible history.

A meteor hit in Russia last night, Mr. Letcher told me when I woke up this morning. And another one, an even bigger one, the size of a football field they said, came very close. Only 20 thousand miles away. They have satellites out, further than that. Did you know that?

Don't they have radar monitoring the solar system? Don't they have billions of dollars' worth of equipment constantly on the lookout for those kinds of things, I asked him?

Of course they do. How do you think they that they spotted the one 20 thousand miles away.

What about the one that hit, why didn't they shoot it down before it entered our atmosphere?

Mr. Letcher was quiet then, and thought about that for several seconds.

I thought the statistical probability of a meteor or asteroid hitting this planet was in the hundreds of billions to begin with. Given the trajectory of the entire universe.

Perhaps, he said, the government, or whoever is in charge, wanted to see what would happen if an automobile sized meteor hit. They have bunkers you see, miles down beneath the surface. They could go down there and live comfortably for 10 to 20 years and then come back up and start all over. I mean, if you think about it, and you are intelligent enough to appreciate it, that is a very appealing idea. You, and two or 3 of your closest friends, and 12 to 15 women, being in a situation to restart the human race. According to just how you see fit.

I wouldn't like it I told him plainly. You haven't thought clearly enough about all of the restrictions that type of situation would impose upon the principles of arousal.

Speaking of arousal, guess what else happened over the weekend, he asked me.

What?

You are going to love this. It is an anomaly worthy of the entire realm of neuroscience.

What is it, I asked him again?

It is right up your alley. It adds to the consistent and meaningful topic of this book. Do you remember in the recent Olympics, the sprinter who didn't have any legs? Who had two spring like mechanisms attached to his mid thighs, and yet, who trained and ran in the Olympics?

Yes I remember him. I do. Vividly, in fact. I was amazed at his success. Medical technology is advancing rapidly.

It is, Mr. Letcher said, then rolled his tongue around his lips, then looked up into the air.

Well, it turns out, that the fellow wrote a book, just like you.

Really, I asked him?

Oh yes, he is in fact, an author. The two of you, are like, two peas in a pod.

That is amazing, I said, what is the book about?

I have no idea, Mr. Letcher said quickly, but over the weekend, it turns out, that the fellow has apparently killed his girlfriend. He is out on bond of course, and is innocent until proven guilty, but I could tell immediately, by his disposition, and attire, that he in fact killed her. Very interesting isn't it?

I was perplexed. Shocked. In disbelief. But, well, as I rolled it around in my head, and began adding up the factors, and imagining different scenarios, slowly, I began to understand the situation.

His girlfriend was an up and coming reality T.V. star, Mr. Letcher said smiling, and they lived in a heavily guarded upscale neighborhood. What do you think about that?

I shall give it much consideration, I told him. It will live with me for the next few years.

How would you feel, if your legs were blown off by a roadside bomb, Mr. Letcher then asked me, given your repertoire for envisioning what other people might be thinking?

I do not believe the situation would be difficult to live with, given enough military and family support. I know from firsthand experience that the onset of P.T.S.D. from combat related factors is relatively light, and natural, compared to the comorbidity that follows from severe childhood physical or sexual abuse, and or abandonment, which factors, especially for adolescent males, generate serial killers, rapists, suicidals, and in the least; drug abusers and the majority of criminals in American Prisons.

But if I was an amputee, or was born without legs, given any set of environmental circumstances, any set, it would most definitely affect my diathesis stress model, and could lead me into a wide range of behaviors, depending on other factors, including murder.

It is late, Mr. Letcher said, and my brain has been acting like a small jumping spider for the last 64 pages. It has not been with me or against me, but has been on the prowl. If you were looking, you have found what you are looking for once again. The end result of using the poorly inadequate little brain to its maximum capacity. The goal of self-control, mastery, attainment, clarity, discipline, all, impostors. The more the brain is used, if it really is used, the more it ends in a strange mixture of fear and displacement. A very high level of fear if the brain is focused on correctly. When you get to the end of the strings that were pulling you, up, and down, and along.

The more I have studied psychology, and neuroscience, the more I wish a wise man would have sat down and talked with me when I was 13 years old, and told me this;

Son, I see myself in your eyes when I was a younger man. I know, that you are yearning for it all, and the whole world seemingly lies open before you. But it is an illusion. All of the aspects of the world are nothing more than the devil vying to use you to seek his own ends. If you want my advice, it is this. Never read anything that does not pertain to your own religion. Go to church. Enjoy the company of your family. Work. Find a job that is physically demanding and work hard. The rewards of a good night's sleep and a loyal wife and children are the highest pleasures that can be achieved on this planet. Nothing, and I mean nothing, supersedes the fulfillment of an honest man who exhausts himself for his family.

I searched the entire world. I studied every religion, philosophy, and way of life known to mankind and indulged in every one of them for a period of time. From all of that, I gained nothing. I have done things that I will not speak of. Things that you can imagine and things that you cannot. My point is this; there is no paradise to find. There are no hidden secrets. Pursuit of the unknown is meaningless, and worse, leads to devastation. A human being was not built to understand this world. Deviation from your basic needs and construction purpose will lead you to misery. A fate, I guarantee, you do not want.

That is what I would have told myself but it is too late. Tonight on the other hand, for the last few hours, I have been busy imagining all of the different ways in which I could kill myself. An old song was playing in my head and I was comforted by the thought of doing it. No matter how bad things get, you can end it all in just one moment. That in itself is comforting me now. Let the bombs and the loud noises go on banging and the voices and the songs and the other two voices and all of it, take it all around, I could nip it all in the bud by just killing myself. Only earlier this evening my head was in fact a large Ferris wheel, and the carnival down below was a dump beyond even a Japanese artist's imagination. I was inside of a room with myself when I was on old man, and the old man had a shotgun and was pointing it at me. The old man was as racist and spiteful as anyone on this planet has ever been. I won't repeat the things that he said as he watched the television, but he almost shot me for them several times. A cat I had found just a year ago where I worked came into the room and he shot it. Splattered it everywhere. Then, a dog I had adopted a few months later came in and he killed it as well. Then there was another person in my head, that was looking in at me through my ear, as if it was a peephole in a door. I walked in on a white room full of the same person multiplied eating rose petals out of cardboard boxes. Another person then took a porcelain toilet and smashed it on the ground, very loudly, then looked at me and said, even that is not enough.

A suit, by itself, making its way around, as if it were worn by an invisible man, but, right when I just wrote that, it held its arms out in defense. No blood in here, he said, just emptiness, and tragedy, that's how I wear it.

So who did you write this for, Heath Letcher asked me? What is the point in writing a book on psychosis? What does that mean psychosis?

It is just a simple word I told him. Easily interchangeable with a dozen others. When I say the triggers of psychosis pulled, I am alluding to the mechanisms of a biological organism being strained. An intended biological function, a human, of a designed organism, the planet, that is analyzing its own neurological processes; via neuroscience, also plans and executes a massacre? Due to inherent evilness? The effects of film and music are greatly unappreciated by modern behavioral psychologists and psychiatrists. The words sociocultural, and psychosocial, are used lavishly and abundantly as a cure all description and final destination for a large variety of disorders that 99.98 percent of psychologists will never understand, but will write off with those 2 words and be finished. No serious clinical trials have ever been thought of or even hinted at on just how much influence some films have upon a person's abilities to think about what is in the best interest of the entire race.

What are the effects of studying abnormal psychology Heath Letcher demanded? Short term and long term? What leads a person into such a field of study to begin with, that is what I want to know. What happens when a person suffering from an axis 1 disorder studies abnormal psychology? What are the potential side effects of completing the program?

What happens when you begin realizing and identifying the childhood instincts and tendencies prevailing in all of the people around you? Does that disassociate you from social capacity?

Are people, like myself, with the gene DRD4-7R; naturally more aggressive, neurochemically speaking? Out of the last 6 mass shootings, how many of the suspects had the gene variant DRD4-7R, just to begin with? How many have been tested genetically? And if so, has significant credibility been given to their genetic make-up?

This new form of psychosis, Mr. Letcher told me, progressive psychosis, is a revolutionary idea in Theoretical physics. We are taking pharmacotherapy as of 2013, and the state of affairs of the entire world, and we are throwing that into a homosexual relationship between Balzac and Camus, a travel guide through India, and a person who asks himself; if I am going to die anyway why not take a bunch of people with me, and all of that is being painted into one picture here, that your organic and prevalent and undisciplined brain is repainting for itself. Painted onto a rolling stem. Like the rain you think you see from behind a two inch thick Plexiglas window and the foggy look of the lights off in the distance before the thorozine kicks in.

The Glass Bottom of the Boat

I am in federal prison isolated under no human contact status. I have 12 consecutive life sentences and have been in prison for 13 years in a cell by myself. I alone am possible of a new transient form of mutilating reality.

In 13 years I have read 1663 books, and an even higher number of journals and newspaper articles and I am only telling you that to introduce you into the pedigree of my artistic capability to design changes in the neural plasticity of a readers mind. Now let me explain to you my self- diagnosis after 13 years in this room by myself. I have at least 5 symptoms for all of the following disorders; post-traumatic stress disorder, generalized anxiety disorder, obsessive compulsive disorder, major bipolar disorder, conversion disorder, depersonalization disorder, dissociative identity disorder, paranoid personality disorder, schizotypal personality disorder, narcissistic and anti-social personality disorder, major anti-social personality disorder and paranoid type schizophrenia.

To be a human being, in the prototypical framework of the average organism has bypassed me. Everything you can imagine has become an unlimited multi-national experience in this little room. I always knew that I had enlarged brain ventricles but did not know what to expect with them until only recently.

Where have you been, Mr. Letcher just asked me?

I am sitting here writing in the dark and can see the electrical impulses of each word firing. In my head, it is like a night on a rough sea in all of this blackness.

What blackness, Mr. Letcher asked me, what has gotten into you?

I was gone for quite some time, I told him. This time I knew I was. I visited my plantation in southeast Georgia, to see how my old friend Vautrin was coming along.

Most of us are living in the 21st century, Mr. Letcher told me. But I see that you like to dwell in the past. Which, I suppose is why you have reinvented me here, which I am glad for, and then he rolled his tongue around his lips, and at the same time, his eyes floated up towards the ceiling. But, he continued, there aren't any small explosives inside my vest. Then he opened his vest up and showed me that it was in fact empty. So what is this string for, and then he tugged on it gently, like he did in the film.

Pull on it and see what happens I told him.

He stared at me for several seconds after I said that.

They made me into that character, he finally stated. Don't you understand that? Can't you comprehend that I was commissioned to make a film in which I did not fully understand the consequences that would take place in society. I had already successfully killed myself once on screen and that impressed them. Someone, somewhere, wanted to push the envelope. They wanted to exploit the creative capacity of my comorbidity. Then he closed his mouth, and then, his jaws suddenly expanded, and then, he reopened his mouth and 3 small snake heads appeared, alive, and in a matter of seconds the snakes came pouring out and as they did, he caught them up quickly and began juggling them. I looked on in complete amazement. He continued juggling the 3, 2 foot long snakes, for about 30 seconds before he caught them all back up with one hand, and then, one at a time, he stuck each one of them back into his mouth and apparently, swallowed them.

I have to give them some fresh air occasionally he said after he finished, in response to the look on my face.

Don't look so surprised he said. That's a trick I learned a long time ago in Calcutta. That's how I would distract the crowd as my nephew made his way through them picking their pockets.

There is a precise algorithm for controlling human behavior. 200 years after Geoffroy Saint-Hilaire realized the differences among the sub groups of the human race clinical trials began on human beings that had been influenced by a sequence of visual and auditory stimulants that had been coded by a mathematical formula received via satellite from deep space. I was a researcher at a university in Colorado studying neuroscience and behavioral neurochemistry on a federal grant when I was kidnapped and brought to this facility and told to write this book. The United States Government is desensitizing you to the inevitability of the future. That you can be controlled and will be. It is integral to an advanced society.

According to an undisclosed document that was slid underneath my cell door;

In a psychophysiological evaluation of Heath Letcher in the film, his micro expressions indicated that he was not in fact, acting the part, but in fact psychobiologically identified with the alleged character, that he was; portraying. Which, in this case study, we have evaluated that he was not, portraying a character, but that he was instead spontaneously expressing core beliefs and ideas. Such micro expressions were cues that perhaps only a few behavioral psychologists could have been aware of. Which were highly authentic, and useful, but contagious given a specific genotype correlation. Then, after massive clinical trials, the story told by the butler; of a sublime and god like savior for mankind in the 21st century, agitated 99.98 percent of study participants beyond capacity and they had to be sedated. The tale of the warlord. The highest mythical archetype for the 22-29 year old North American male in the year 2013. One idea now superimposing another. Told by the mentor/parental archetype warning the protagonist that his enemy had left diamonds, rubies, and emeralds, the size of acorns, scattered on the ground in his camp. Such items having no value to a savage, who robbed and murdered, not out of greed, but out of sport.

Here we have a North American prototype of Kali. For 100 million viewers to witness committing innumerable terroristic acts, robbing banks, murdering randomly and at will, kidnapping and killing hostages, including high ranking politicians, throwing women off of skyscrapers, blowing up a hospital, blowing up a police station, and finally in a complete act of open aggression against global society, setting approximately 75 million dollars on fire. Because some men just want to see the world burn, like myself.

According to the final evaluation of the report, there was a three way shifting perspective of protagonistic/antagonistic qualities of the films 3 component personalities, a perfect triangle, which is key to the algorithm. Out of the three, the hero, deemed so by the viewers after clinical trials, explained that in order to move forward in a frivolous and unworthy society one had to break the established rules. All of them. And essentially, to follow his example. Which, according to the document, 5 percent of the male viewers in North America engaged in some form of serious criminal activity 1-5 days after watching the film. With .08 percent committing murder.

What do you believe in exactly, Mr. Letcher asked me just now? And are you still in a cell by yourself, imagining all of this?

Are you in fact still in an institution or aren't you, Jisoo Kim wanted to know?

What is your name? Why do you always try to change the subject when I ask you what your name is?

Psychopathy Revisited.

If there was a line, Heath Letcher informed me calmly, you have obviously crossed it.

Then, he just stared at me for several minutes.

Do you think that you can just turn around and go back to where ever it is that you came from?

The invisible man in the suit shrugged his shoulders.

Is there a cure for psychopathy I asked him?

According to the latest abnormal psychology textbook there is not a cure for either psychopathy or anti-social personality disorder.

Is there a cure for schizophrenia , the paranoid type, which has caused me to write, an elaborate delusional theory that the government and a few Hollywood directors are directly influencing, albeit unknowingly, mass shootings.

There is medication to reduce the symptoms, but there is no cure. But, I would also like to add, that, perhaps you are not as delusional as you think you are. Although clearly you are a psychopath, or one that is affected by psychopathy.

Heath Letcher was wearing his purple suit, and had just put on a fresh coat of makeup and eyeliner.

You are still obsessed by the latest mass shooting Jisoo Kim said, staring into my eyes.

I am, I admitted.

And if you hadn't been caught, you would have done something as well wouldn't you have?

You would have harmed someone, and possibly yourself?

That is correct, I told her.

Have you continued to write about your feelings, she asked me next? Have you been keeping a journal like I asked you?

I have.

Writing is very therapeutic. The actual term to describe it is as transpsychological. Or a transpsychological outlet. Being aware of your own thoughts, and emotions, promotes balance and wholeness with your environment. Have you found writing in your journal helpful? Does it release your negative and analytical feelings?

I don't know yet, I told her.

Well, do you still the think about the shooting very often?

I have never particularly dwelled on it, but I still think about it from time to time.

What about the daydreams you described to me last month? Where you told me about how you continuously fantasized about killing large groups of people with an assault rifle. One scenario you described was a group of correctional officers in the parking lot here at this institution at shift change. You told me that you thought you could kill 20-30 of them if you had two assault rifles with 70 round drums and multiple 30 round clips. Another scenario you described was attacking the county courthouse that sent you here. Another scenario was kidnapping the sheriff of that county and dragging him on a chain behind your truck. Were you just upset that day last month, or were, are, these daydreams actually prototypical?

I constantly fantasize about; what you would term anti-social behavior, but the subgroups of people that I would prefer to attack change almost daily. Most recently I thought about attacking an award show for films.

Why, she asked me?

Because the actors and directors spend hundreds of thousands of dollars on their clothing and jewelry while half of the world suffers from malnourishment.

If released, do you think that you would ever act out on any of these fantasies?

No. Because what I have studied about my various disorders, and what you have told me, leads me to believe that I am just seeking attention, and that I am basically self-centered and very childish, and love acting like a 5 year old.

It is a shame that your intelligence is going to such a waste, Jisoo Kim told me. But it is not surprising; the smartest two people I have ever met were also paranoid type schizophrenics. In the end, you will die, alone, and useless, in some institution. How does that make you feel?

I do not believe that, I told her. Just now, for example, I had an impulse to smash the side of your face in for saying that, but I resisted it. Because I do in fact want to be released, and lead a normal life. A peaceful life. I can imagine myself as cured.

She then jotted down some notes on her pad, and she readjusted her legs as she did so.

There is no cure for psychopathy, she told me. But, never the less, your release date is quickly approaching, and so I would just like you to know that, although you have made some small amount of progress, the odds of you adapting to, and functioning in, modern American society, are probably in the millions. I would have a better chance of buying a quick pick lottery ticket this evening and winning 250 million dollars tomorrow morning.

What about Heath Letcher, she then asked me. Do you still talk to him?

Don't answer that question, the invisible man in the suit told me. The fact that you have imagined all of this to begin with, ergo; a dead actor brought back to life as a character in a novel written by a severely mentally ill inmate inside of an institution about another mentally ill inmate who is guided by an invisible psychiatrist in a white linen suit is downright harrowing. The henchmen of law enforcement in this country won't allow it. The entire system of this country was built upon the idea of English Aristocracy instilling morality upon their peasants. That system was not created to recognize and diagnose psychobiological processes and patterns in human behavior. Who do you think you are, Dorothea Dix? And then the man in the invisible suit laughed. They will have you killed. Your gaze pattern over the last 10 seconds suggests that you are in agreement with what I just said. What do you think that you are writing even as I am saying this? Do you think that this will be brushed off as a satire? Do you think that you can write down that you have fantasized about killing a large group of correctional officers, and I did, and that, an average working middle class American is going to find that amusing, or insightful?

Chuck Phallanuik wrote a novel where the main character started a terrorist organization and subsequently blew up 12 skyscrapers belonging to various financial institutions, I told him.

That is different, the invisible man in the strait jacket said. That is highly different. People aren't blowing up buildings to erase the debt crises, but there have been several mass shootings. And here you are saying that you want to go out and kill a group of people also.

No, that is not what I am saying. What I have been trying to say all along is this; there is a reason why James Holves killed 12 people and injured a hundred more. There is a psychobiological reason why every mass shooting, beginning with colombine to my memory, has happened.

There are reasons for these anomalies.

There were patterns of behavior that progressed up into the incidents, due, entirely, to environmental factors, throughout the life span of the organism.

A human being is a biological, mechanism, and is subject to billions of untested stimuli beginning in childhood. No single psychiatrist or psychologist or biologist or computer program understands the neurological development of every single person on the planet, much less the government officials that write the laws and the personnel they have enforcing them. The entire criminal justice system of this country needs to be abolished. The advancements made in neurochemistry and behavioral psychology in the last 60 years have been in vain, for as ignorant as 99.98 percent of the population of this country is.

You realize, the invisible man in the suit said,(in the darkness), that you are biased because you are in an institution yourself, and are in administrative segregation because of your conduct in the institution, and that if you were a typical middle class American drinking your beer and watching a football game you wouldn't even begin to care about who was locked up, or where, or for what reason, nor would you care about the underlying reasons of the latest mass shooting as long as the shooter was now dead or in jail waiting to die and moreover you would approve of whatever the government wanted to do in any situation so long as you could go on drinking your beer, consuming enough food for 3 people daily, and watching films and listening to music that catered to your consistently naive pleasure seeking lifestyle. Guided almost 90 percent pre dominantly by your right brain functions. Your left brain analytical skills having been isolated and rendered obsolete by your 17th or 18th year of life in this country. You realize that don't you?

I do, I told him. I really do. I understand the situation, and the concept that people are as they have been formed. But how many people understand that if a person is a clinical psychopath, or has severe anti-social personality disorder, or paranoid type schizophrenia; that there are only a few neurological triggers that need to be pulled and a massacre, or a single incident of murder, is only a natural biological reaction of a human being given a subset of environmental circumstances.

It is dangerous to say that, Heath Letcher told me. You have gone entirely too far.

I have been in a cell by myself for 8 years, I told him. Do you expect me to be happy about that, or pleased? Do you think that I was actually rehabilitated? Did you think that after 8 years of incarceration and the environment of violence therein that I wouldn't have reached an altered state in my psychopathy given my childhood exposure to not only severe neglect and abuse but also strands of eastern philosophy which has aided and abetted my psychopathy into an evolving form. I can't help but to feel special, because I was a psychopath, but I cured myself. Through diaphragmatic breathing, inclusive meditation, and using positive mental imagery and visualizing that I could still have a successful career in this world as a writer. Given the fact that I used journal writing as a means to reduce the symptoms of my mental illnesses. I feel particularly special and narcissistic about that. Do you see how the symptoms of my disorders come and go? That is a sign that I am recovering, and can still be used as an element in a family setting, given the chance.

Folie A Deux

My assignment was to directly influence approximately 60 to 80 thousand people into a shared psychotic disorder. That is a disorder where one person shares the delusions of someone whom they have had a close personal relationship with who is delusional. That is what is happening to you. Once my delusions are in your head as even being remotely in significance with reality, you have a variation of schizophrenia known as a shared psychotic disorder.

This is a behavioral learning experiment. If someone somewhere still thinks that this is a novel, or that this is entertaining, they have a variation of schizophrenia worse than the variety that I am suffering from. There are two concepts at work here presently, Mr. Letcher explained to me; cognitive restructuring and behavior modification. Recently, I finished reading the book that I wrote 4 years ago. The one involving Kevin Childs. How disturbing, I thought to myself. I realized, when I finished reading that book, just how toxic my personality is. I never understood so previously. Is the same pattern of behavior present here? What have I done to myself I asked Mr. Letcher? What is wrong with me? It is all in the approach, he told me. Your approach is very unbalanced. The lines shaping your, self-image, are very uneven.

I have worked with several psychiatrists on these issues, I told him.

Jisoo Kim, in the beginning of one of our first sessions, explained to me that; the fact that I wanted to be cured, was one of the key factors, perhaps the most important, if it was even possible that I could be cured.

Now, given the aptitude of what I have studied, and, the usage of a multi- dimensional approach to cognitive functioning that I have presented you with, I believe that you should take what I am saying seriously. I am a psychopath, and now you are a psychopath. The abnormal psychology textbook proves it.

In comparison to previous documents that I have written, can you see the difficult transition I have made? I no longer use profanity. The overall tone is more dignified, and respectful. Perhaps I have become more optimistic. Perhaps, a psychopath can be cured.

GOKUDO

What could a civilian possibly know about what drives a person to murder someone, Heath Letcher asked me?

What do you mean by civilian I asked him?

The trash that's around us. With their unassuming and unskeptical pretentiousness. And here's this book that some fool wrote about martyrs, suicide bombers, and mass shooters, which, apparently he thinks are all under the same demographic subset, and just take a look at it. He showed me the book. I wish I could get a whole group of such people together; people that think that they know something about the qualities, or uncharacteristic qualities, of a mass shooter, and line them up and shoot them. That would be appropriate, and allowable, under our standards, wouldn't it? Then he stared at me for several moments waiting for my response.

I think that perhaps only you and I have an idea about what type of person studies for, and pursues a career as; either a psychiatrist, or a neuroscientist. A very abnormal and unnatural person is what type of person I am referring to, who would prefer to stare at cat scans, pet scans, and FMRIs all day long for several years, than sell cars. Or dwell upon the reasons for, and the symptoms of, more than a hundred plus varieties of mental disorders, than take pictures of naked women for a living. Or would prefer to spend 8 hours a day with their mentally ill patients for several years, when

they know well the extents of a shared psychotic disorder. I just
wonder what type of person could continuously review literally
thousands of symptoms in the DSM5 and not wonder about their
own neurological similarities to such symptoms constantly. Perhaps,
what I am insinuating is that most doctorate level psychiatrists and
or neuroscientists have pathological symptoms that led them to
study such fields of science out of a reliability to their own personal
belief that they could cure themselves. Obviously a dozen or so
personnel in the pentagon know what I am getting at. Although I
am not really getting at it am I? Because I know, with certainty, that
no matter how many case studies I read and then reread, or how
many gene variants they find and eliminate in my DNA, or for how
many months I take chlorpromazine, in the end, I see now that my
path is leading in only one direction. The direct opposite from
where the other dozen in the 5 sides are leading them. Is it driven
psychobiologically, was it out of my hands to begin with? No, it was
triggered. Clearly I was afflicted with Dissociative Identity Disorder,
and so was my friend Mr. Nolman. Take Bain for example. The same
person also starred in a film titled Brunsen. That is in fact what
drove me to write this book. I am infatuated with the idea of
modern acting. Just think about it. Seemingly average young people
who are seen out in public riding their bicycles, or outside of a
coffee shop chitchatting with a friend, or at an award show smiling
pleasantly, dressed fantastically, these wonderful and good looking

young people being capable of such powerful character transformation is frightening from a psychological standpoint.

Personally, I am inspired by such performances. It makes me want to take the idea of transformation to its utmost extreme. By writing all of this, having made all of this up out of the blue, but then turning out to be actually very normal and well behaved. I have all along just been describing my symptoms for my psychiatrist to be able to better diagnose me. I hope that no one else ever reads this, or if anyone does that they just laugh it off. I use to be a psychiatrist myself before I began my regimen of anti-psychotic medication, and anti-depressants. At one point I had everything in the world a man could want but it wasn't good enough. Before I began the medication trials there was nothing wrong with me, nothing, but I couldn't see myself prescribing someone a particular drug without knowing what it was like to take it myself. It just wouldn't be fair, I thought. So I began by trying all of the first generation anti psychotics. Chlorpromazene two days a week and haloperdul two days a week. Then molendone and fluphenazene together two days a week. Then perhenazene on Sundays and I did that for 6 months while I locked myself away in my basement. Then, I woke up one morning and decided to start on the second generation of anti-psychotics. I started with quetiavine, which I enjoyed thoroughly. Then I tried arpiprazole and risperadone. Then ziprasedone and clozavine. But out of all the anti-psychotics I particularly liked the thorazene and the seriquils the most. The anti-depressants, especially the SSRIs, the SNRIs, the tricyclics, and the MAOIs were all a waste of time and I wouldn't have ever prescribed them to anybody. Having trouble sleeping or feeling anxious are you? I'd quickly prescribe my patient 900 mg of thorazene a day, and 750 mg of seriquil at night. Then they were cured. In most cases I would never even see or hear from the patient again. The only anti-depressants that even remotely made me feel anything were the bupropons, and that only happened when I crushed them up and snorted them.

Now, as to my benzodiazapam regimens? 10 mg valums taken 3 at a time are the cure all for that little group. I also experimented with lithium and neurotens, which, I, at one point was taking 4000 mg of neuroten every day before I switched over to my methamphetamine addiction, which, I was averaging about 5-10 grams a day before I was brought to this institution. I really was.

I always knew that my variety of Dissociative identity disorder was progressive. My psychiatrist Heath Letcher told me that when I first met him and we began discussing our psychiatric treatments, that I would gradually become more aware of my differing periods of disassociation. It was because of the transcranial electromagnetic stimulation therapy, I was told. I was subverted in an uncharacteristic manner during these sessions. I was sure that I

wasn't in the process of derealization. I was positive of that.
Although, the TES did cure me of my D.I.D., the side effect was that
in the process I picked up depersonalization disorder. Thousands of
times when I was alone in the isolation cell I distinctly knew that I
was floating in the middle of the room. I noticed subtle and even
occasionally sudden changes in the water pressure coming out of
my sink, although I was assured that no such changes in water
pressure occurred because it was closely monitored.

Everything felt discontinuous in that room.

If I was breathing the room was also breathing and you will never
understand that I guarantee you until you are in isolation for
several years. The room imitated my behavior. It was larger than
the sky at 2 o clock in the afternoon staring straight up at a single
white cloud. I have went on and on for years where it was all unreal
fugue. My psychiatrist began using phrases such as, the feeling
puzzles the experiencer. Or, I was referred to as an automaton. I
was told that my delusional theories on modern cinema controlling
35 percent of the populations behavior patterns was attenuating
my delusion that I was living in a movie myself or was a character in
a book that I was writing and nothing more. That the organism was
separate from the material.

Your own comorbidity is astounding you, Jisoo Kim told me. I am
going to need you to continue writing in your journal as it will make

for an excellent case study. There has been very little research done, perhaps there hasn't been any, on the intensity of the confusion that you have been reporting. Whether or not you are experiencing these delusions or are simply imagining that you are experiencing them, I do not think matters at this point.

Perhaps, I'm an artist, I offered in response. Wouldn't it be wonderful if all of this was a product of my creative transitivity?

That is another one of your delusions she told me. No artist, or filmmaker, or writer, has the capacity to augment or portray experiences which they have no personal familiarity with. On the contrary human beings talk about, and act upon, events and experiences that they have an episodic, semantic, or procedural memory of. That and nothing more.

Even if I have studied more psychological concepts than anyone in the history of the world?

That is another delusion she said.

She probably doesn't even know the difference between being an alter identity or a mother/wife archetype, Mr. Letcher mentioned, and yet she knows what a delusion is, and then he laughed. And if you understand what I just said then I feel sorry for you.

I can't help but wonder how a psychiatrist or a curious mid-level psychologist couldn't help but to find D.I.D., extremely amusing and not want to act as if they had the disorder just from studying it so intensely, I asked her?

Your etiology, which formed from extremely long periods of intense incarceration, should be classified as a completely new disorder, Jisoo Kim stated after she thought about it for several minutes. There is no organic basis. The identities of your D.I.D. appear to be a bit more integrated than what I have previously studied. Yet they are all psychopathic, and have depleted their emotional responses out of sheer fascination with psychological case studies. And the more I look at you, and think about the things you say, and think about you sitting there reading this, the more I find myself wanting to smile.

I know that I am sick, but I am aware of it.

It's because you want to push everything to the extreme, Heath Letcher commented, just like I did. Then;

GOKUDO! Heath Letcher shouted right in the middle of the unit!

They know absolutely nothing!

If I could have flown a plane into an aircraft carrier I would have done that too! If I could have strapped a bomb around my torso and walked up to a police check point I would have done that too. An AR 15, modern guerilla warfare, you think you know what it takes, they're lucky they caught me when they did.

GOKUDO! Heath Letcher shouted again and then he was subdued, and drug away.

The sun is high and my brain is small, but it is very wet.

That is haiku directly from my padded isolation cell, Mr. Letcher told me, presumably, where I was left at the end of the film.

Determinism, Jisoo Kim said. That is the word that would describe the general outlook of your fetish. Basically you are frustrated with a predominately uneducated society that doesn't understand that all behaviors are the result of identifiable causes, even if the causes are not immediately apparent, or clear.

That is correct I told her.

But then you incorrectly assume that by outlining your complaints against the above mentioned society, and/or, then attacking and killing a small group of its members, that you will have a personal effect on, or cause a change in, a proportion of that societies behavioral or cognitive patterns.

I was struck by the obviously flawed outlook I had generated. And, distinctly, I remember, I felt remorseful for what I had written, and ashamed, and instantly I felt suicidal.

Even a military psychiatrist, Jisoo Kim continued, who was scrutinized in every psychological manner conceivable prior to his employment, succumbed to bi-directional influences and went on a rampage. So do not overly antagonize yourself. Everyone is susceptible to psychosocial influences. The important idea to remember here is to realize that less than 1 percent of the global population study psychology, and a smaller percentage of that subgroup study behavioral psychology in all of its implications exclusively. Determinism, as a concept, is generally unacceptable by the American population because of the prevalent belief in free will, religious philosophies, and the general socioeconomic culture of individualism. All of which are absurd and unsustainable assumptions that if willingly researched would be found to have no credible scientific basis, or value, to the long term sustainability of this planet. What you have written on the other hand has a high heuristic quality although I have no idea who it will benefit or in what way it will benefit them as I do not like to assume like most people. As to your therapy, I believe that you are making progress. Your journal writing, likewise, is making progress. It exists in and of itself, separate from the breathing organism. Perhaps you could begin to think about new ways to channel your observations about society, positive or negative, into constructive writing essays that would bring about beneficial changes in the behavior patterns of the people you encounter, as opposed to shoot, or blow up, people who do not understand behavioral psychology and/or psychobiological processes who in your opinion are naive and selfish but in reality just don't know better.

Heath Letcher told me that I shouldn't succumb to such nonviolent methods, that, there was no glory in it, and the invisible man in the suit, moreover, said that a government that had no prerequisite requirements of behavioral studies for its highest ranking politicians didn't deserve to be bargained with. According to my psychiatrist though, they just don't know better, I told them, and they both shrugged. The more I think about it in fact, and I did think about it, these people that you and I would gladly see dead, are not people in the sense that we think they are; as having a choice in the outcome of their personality. They are biological mechanisms that are part of a larger biological organism. That with the correct amount of information given, have behavioral patterns that are 100 percent predictable. If I can accurately predict what a person is going to say or do, or if I know exactly what it is that they are thinking, or feeling, how can I possibly hate or despise such a simple biological organism? I just came to that conclusion this evening.

I too now believe that I can contribute to society in accord with the patterns of acceptable behavior, which I had previously learned but now have a better understanding of, in conjunction with the desires I am manifesting to become a successful writer, which I know also stems from one of my personality disorders. Which, I think I now have a cure for as well. I could burn this book without anyone ever reading it. Imagine the tremendous satisfaction I would feel if I burned this book and then never tell anyone I wrote it. I once wrote a book that was perhaps grandiose and epic, and I burned it, along with two other books I wrote. That is how I fixed myself, and why I am typing this now. 6 years of my most imaginative writing was sacrificed for this small stack of paper.

I have substituted the need for stimulation, Mr. Letcher told me. Essentially, I was forced to.

I am merely an observer, and am not ahead of the curve as I stated previously.

Although I have written many portentous and ghastly sections in this book I am at base an altruistic human being and passionately want to see other people do well. My concern is that the world is severely inefficient in stimulating my need for arousal, up to the appropriate level.

I would like to have a more interesting job. That is the actual reason why I wrote this short essay. I would not discriminate between any employers or job descriptions so long as I was essentially, given what I am looking for.

I have not written this pamphlet to provoke any type of maladaptive behavior in any one. On the contrary I have tried to illuminate what types of conditions are prevalent in the minds of psychopaths, that, I have spent a predominately long period of time around. To which, a person such as yourself must admit, that I have risen above the urges of accommodation to my environment.

I am 29 years old and have spent most of the last 15 years in an institution and have heard thousands of personal stories of heinous crimes and have seen hundreds of incidents take place before my very eyes, including suicide and murder. Writing was in fact my mode for releasing toxic stimulants. Most of which, those documents I destroyed myself, some pieces of paper I consumed literally.

I have spent long periods of time alone in severely traumatizing sensory deprived isolation cells, beginning when I was 16, in a juvenile detention center. I have stated this yet again for my own benefit, to relax myself. As writing about my own experiences and how I feel about them, I can almost say evidently effects a vast amount of the neurotransmitters in my head. Hence the need for stimulation, to replace those memories. Which is the key to human motivation.

NO HISTORY

It's not them, or they, Heath Letcher told me, they are not there selves. Don't even look at them as people, or the epitome of people. Earlier today, let me strain for a moment, an elderly gentlemen was reading a newspaper. Which disturbed me because I had never before witnessed this particular individual reading the newspaper but instead, on numerous occasions, perhaps hundreds of times, I had seen him reading a celebrity gossip magazine. So I asked this person why he was reading a newspaper all of a sudden, and he made a comment to the extent of; "you thought you had me figured out didn't you slick".

Where upon, I informed him that I did not, and would not, tolerate new forms of behavior in my immediate environment. That such new behaviors would make me wonder about things, and that, essentially, I wouldn't be able to concentrate if I was thinking.

I then asked Mr. Letcher how he thought he had come to be here?

Everything is constantly being replaced he told me. Presumably, I died years ago, but I have simply been updated by the phase sequences in that lump of communal tissue, that you call your head.

Actually, Mr. Letcher told me, I was hired by a pharmaceutical company to test a new drug for amnesiacs and brain trauma patients. In a nutshell, the drug that we were testing had an unprecedented effect on a particular group of neurotransmitters which wiped out the test subjects episodic memory, completely. The semantic memory on the other hand having been left completely intact.

Brainwashing, in as much as, is in fact only a dozen years away he told me. No History, LTD, will be the name of this, our, company.

Let's talk about categories, I then suggested.

What do you want to know exactly he asked me?

What are the triggers of neural assemblies?

Arousal he said quickly.

What is scaffolding I asked him next?

What you have done here, and then he did a little skip into the air and giggled.

What is parallel distributed processing I asked him?

The theory that no one region, or lobe, or assembly, or sequence, in your brain is in control of the entire process. There are perhaps patterns of activation that occur more frequently than others, but no consistent amount of information yet on the given triggers that activate behavior. Every day 88 billion neurons have been involved in the results of this book. Which when reread has caused the writer to feel disassociated from the material. How is it possible to be shocked at one's own behavior without even distribution spread out across the various brain regions. This happens all the time, and is proof that there is no central organization and that neural activity is much more primitive than modern human ruling class idealism suggests.

Decay theory, and displacement theory, explain how you might have forgotten how you felt about the world a year ago, what you were reading, activities you were partaking in, and what you were writing. It is plausible that as advanced as you motivate yourself to think you are you have forgotten most of the theories for the basis of that motivation rapidly. Only the impression is left. Which is itself an electrically charged chemical substance and nothing more. Recent events further suggest that even a bachelor's degree, master's degree, and an almost obtained doctorate in neuroscience are not much in the way either of helping an individual to understand their own tendencies. Generally, I'll throw this out there, the majority of psychologists, psychiatrists, and neuroscientists are people who suffer from mental disorders and who are seeking information on treating or curing their own symptoms.

All of science in modern global society is a shared psychotic disorder Heath Letcher told me. An education is only a model of endless metaphors, and then he licked his lips before he added, people are strings of neurons and nothing more.

When the chips get low, they, will, resort to any and all forms of new behaviors previously unimaginable. Which is to say that the activation of any specific assembly will correspond exactly to the stimulation of the environment.

If I had no history in the film, for example, if I appeared suddenly and seemingly out of nowhere as a psychopath who could destroy all of the underlying aspects of society, I, the joker, the apex of all criminal masterminds, if I could appear suddenly out of a void and collapse an entire society, similarly, mental disorders could appear out of nowhere in the viewers who had witnessed me engaging in my maladaptive behavior pattern who themselves had no previous history of a mental disorder. Do you have access to an internet search engine? Cross reference everything I have just said Heath Letcher told me.

Cross reference imitation.

Cross reference the need for stimulation.

Cross reference sources of arousal.

I want you personally, to extensively study all research that has taken place on sensory deprivation and/or sensory deprivations on the effects of arousal theory and behavioral restructuring.

What does the phrase; Social Learning, mean?

How many politicians know who Albert Bandura is?

Tell the reader one last time, Mr. Letcher told me, that is has been proven, that human learning, or observational learning, results from imitating models.

I have to remind you of that, because I understand the limits of human memory and how uninteresting the concept of prolonged self-analysis must be for the majority of the population. I am just reminding you that learning results from imitating models. As advanced as you think the world is, or human animals are, it, they, is, are, not. We live in an era where films such as Mr. Nolman's Dark Night are released and people assumed the behavior of the antagonist wouldn't be imitated. Why, I do not know. It is especially amusing to me because research studies as early as the 1980s had already proved that maladaptive behavior patterns viewed in films would in fact be precisely modeled.

Type; Evans, 1989, into your database and see how that fits into your model of the underlying structures of a progressively altruistic human society. Which doesn't yet exist.

People, respond to their environment. People, do not have internal beliefs, feelings, or desires, without stimulants from their environment causing such responses. Just because the pleasure seeking and naive upper class American society frowns upon behavioristic theories, does not mean such theories are not true.

Think logically, Heath Letcher urged me. Think kindly. The level of violence has remained isolated to a very small percentage of the American population. Since your view is biased, think about the potential effects of what you are about to write. Wait 15 seconds, then respond.

I am, just, maybe, smart enough to understand the functional necessity of government in society, and the tremendous amount of pressure put upon such individuals to react to situations dealing with group psychology. Even though, in actuality, the entire country, every single person included, as units of a massive environmental structure, are to blame for the mass shootings just as much as the shooters, which perhaps only 5 people will understand, well, in short, given everything that I have written here, I will cut to the chase and simply ask if I can have permission and federal funding to open my own research facility and be given approximately 2 thousand convicted criminals to experiment on in my new behavioral restructuring program. I would like to conduct a massive research study on such individuals. Preferably, I would like to have 5 thousand individuals as I have multiple experiments that I want to research extensively. Half of the test subjects would need to be volunteers, the other half, unwilling volunteers. Then, give me 5 years and the results of my experiments, I absolutely guarantee you, will unrattle your previously solid foundations and beliefs about the human condition.

Behavior can be structured, and biochemically restructured.

The current methods of incarceration employed by the government are inefficient due to a lack of awareness about the reality of Human Behavior. Modern government imitates its representatives. Which are unprepared for what the next 20 years has in store for them, unless they give me a facility.

No, Heath Letcher said, I didn't fall, I threw myself down on to the cement head first.

All in an instant I viddied thrashing and ripping away and tearing my own skin off and mashing it down on to the paper tablet and smearing it around all over this cell and then, I even dug one of my own eyeballs out and smashed it down on to this page also, and then I took it, and smeared it all over the padding in here as well. I'll paint that on a canvas also.

When I am finished with the painting, I will show it to Mr. Letcher, and as he looks at it we will discuss the lie detector tests, brain scans, and truth serums being used to determine if the fellow from Colorado was in fact legally insane. But as to whether Mr. Nolman was legally insane, or is, not one out of 7 billion are concerned with.

But don't misunderstand me, or think about this for more than ten seconds, layers down in my brain tissue I am pleased with everything that has been transpiring. It has been an orchestra of nobility and intrigue.

Mr. Letcher himself, on this particular day was dressed fashionably in a white linen suit, tailored, and had on a blood red silk tie. Every time he opened his mouth to pronounce electrical poetry a dead Circadian was lying on his tongue as he spoke.

I am an exhibionist, Mr. Letcher told me. This has been my show. Writing is my fetish, and I am grateful to have been able to simulate my diversity here. Given the chance, for example, these new suits that I have been hearing about, that a defense contractor has been working on for the military, if I could get my hands on one of those suits, and a fleet of armed drones, what I am saying is; I enjoy all of this so much, I could, I am, I'm dancing to it. This is me dancing in response to the rampage that happened just a few days ago in California. I wish it would have been myself shot to pieces, in a morgue somewhere, it couldn't be any worse than the morgue I'm in now. But I am dancing and singing, and I am happy about everything there is. I am sure that a lot of people are disillusioned, Mr. Letcher told me privately. But I am so exuberant I could burst, because every person I have killed is inside me, and then he smiled. Every person has value.

Swishhhh, and then, Swashhhh, goes the blood underneath my head. A hot cup of coffee. Knowing exactly 2 of the last people you were. A concerto by Chopin early in the morning. And then this, making your own brain laugh.

Now, you have it. Mr. Letcher patted me on the knee and told me. He patted my knee as my grandfather might have. You have what I have and you'll end up doing something very, extreme. Now won't you? And then he giggled.

You're as pale as old Saint Squat. You remind me of someone who likes to go a cemetery and walk around in circles for hours. And if a raven should fly over your head, you would swear by your green candle that it meant something.

When I was younger, Mr. Letcher went on, I got drunk one night and went to a graveyard and dug up a coffin randomly. It took me almost 3 hours. I had found an abandoned shack in the woods a mile away from my grandfather's house, and I took the skeleton to that wooden shack. I sat it up in a chair and put one of my grandfather's suits on it. Then, a few days later, I began talking to it.

You can contact the author by email at

lionsden.head88@yahoo.com

www.ingramcontent.com/pod-product-compliance
Lightning Source LLC
Chambersburg PA
CBHW071524170626
46811CB00007B/2948